17 mistakes in 201 pap.!

W9-DDL-877

WITHDRAWN

SAPPHIRE

A Grandmother's Rings Romance

SAPPHIRE

•

Kathryn Quick

AVALON BOOKS
NEW YORK

Published by Thomas Bouregy & Co., Inc.
160 Madison Avenue, New York, NY 10016

Library of Congress Cataloging-in-Publication Data

Quick, Kathryn.
   Sapphire / Kathryn Quick.
        p. cm.
   ISBN 978-0-8034-9983-6 (hardcover)
   1. Weddings—Fiction.   2. New Jersey—Fiction.   I. Title.
   PS3567.U2935S27 2009
   813'.54—dc22

                                                    2009025434

PRINTED IN THE UNITED STATES OF AMERICA
ON ACID-FREE PAPER
BY HADDON CRAFTSMEN, BLOOMSBURG, PENNSYLVANIA

For Mom

Thanks to my husband, Don, who understood that I needed to write before I cooked dinner some days. Love you to the moon and back. Xoxoxoxoxo

Chapter One

"This is all your fault!"

His sister's words stopped Trent Archer from opening the front door to St. Mary's Catholic Church. He removed his hand from the ornate brass handle and looked down at her. She stood five steps below him, arms crossed in front of her, looking as though she were going to have to be carried inside.

"My fault?" Trent asked, putting a hand on his chest, honestly surprised at the accusation. "How do you figure that?"

Ali Archer's eyes narrowed. "Our sister is getting married to your friend." She poked her finger at him. "*Your* friend, your *fault*," she shot back.

Trent held up his hands in a defensive gesture. "Not mine. If it's anyone's fault, it's Mom's." He lowered his hands and walked down the five steps to her. "And if it's Mom's fault, it's your fault. You had all that time with her before she gave us each one of Grandmother's rings with all that maternal voodoo attached." He threw his hands up in the air and waved them as he spoke. *"I want grandchildren and these rings will help you find your soul mates,"* he mimicked. "Then like magic Somer met Nick and before any of us knew what hit us, they're getting married."

Ali crossed her arms over her chest. "Maybe this year for Christmas we should get Mom a cauldron she can stir."

"Not funny, Mooch."

Ali glared at him. "Try moving beyond nicknames for a while, will you?"

"Sorry. Old habits die hard."

"The fact remains that since Mom gave us those rings, things have changed." She tossed her head. "Where did you put yours?"

Trent shrugged. "In my dresser somewhere. With my socks, I think. What about you?"

"I rented a safe-deposit box and stuck it in there. Behind all that steel and concrete, nothing can get out."

"We can only hope."

"Yeah, like your socks are going to protect you from Mom's love-voodoo."

"Mooch . . ."

"It's Ali," she corrected, pointing at him. "Allamuchy to be exact. Named after a state park by flower-child parents of the seventies, remember *Trenton*?" Ali rolled her eyes. "And if Somer and Nick have children, I wonder if they'll continue Mom's quirky tradition of naming their babies after the place in which they were planned."

"Lordy, I hope not. Can you imagine if they decide to have a baby right away? Like on their honeymoon?" Trent cradled an imaginary child in his arms. "Oh, little Hawaii Daultry. Isn't he cute?"

"Heaven forbid," Ali agreed. "I can only imagine the nicknames."

"I'm sure Somerville wouldn't do that to her offspring."

"Who knows what she'll do. She's all sentimental and romantic these days." Ali narrowed her eyes. "It's the rings, I tell you. Stay as far away from them as you can."

Trent nodded and did some finger-pointing of his own. "Maybe you should have hidden the rings before we got to Mom's that day."

"How was I supposed to know she was going to pull them out and curse us with them?" Ali said in her own defense.

"Because you're the baby of the family, and historically the younger child is always closest to the mother."

"Well, I had no idea that Grandma put some hex on the rings, or that you were going to leave our sister alone with some guy who would sweep her off her feet and have her registering at Macy's for wedding gifts before we could stop it."

Trent's jaw tightened. "I was working at the time Somer met Nick."

"If that's what you call driving around in a police cruiser all day waiting for someone to run a red light."

"Mooch, that's not all I do and you know it."

"Stop calling me that." Ali waved her hands in front of her face. "Never mind." She looked at her watch. "It's bad enough that we got roped into being in the wedding party, and now we're late."

"So then stop yammering and let's get in there."

Ali began to walk up the church steps and then stopped. She turned to her brother. "Wait. We're not going in there until we make a pact."

Trent's brows furrowed. "What kind of pact?"

Ali held up her hand and made a fist, crooking her little finger at Trent. "No matter what, we are not going to let Grandmother's rings get us. Deal?"

Trent smiled. "Not if I can help it." He hooked his pinky around hers. "Deal." With the pact firmly sealed with a pinky promise, he gestured toward the looming church doors. "Now let's get this rehearsal thing over with. Weddings give me the creeps."

The wind caught the door of the church as it opened, sending it crashing against the brick wall and announcing the arrival of the latecomers. Linda Wolff, until now the only partnerless bridesmaid, turned toward the sound along with the twelve other people in the vestibule. She brushed her dark hair from her eyes and looked at the couple that entered. They were bickering about something.

Somer Archer, tomorrow's bride, left the groom's side and hurried toward them. "Trent, Ali, you made it. Now we can start the rehearsal."

"It's her fault that we're late," Linda heard the tall, sandy-haired man say. "You know Ali. She had to get in the last word before we came in here." There was unmistakable annoyance in his tone.

Nick Daultry, the groom, walked over and clapped the man's shoulder. "I believe you," he said. Nick turned and motioned to Linda. "Come on over so I can make formal introductions."

Great, Linda thought, watching Somer embrace the pair as she walked to them. *Mr. Happy must be my partner.*

Nick caught Linda's elbow in his free hand. "Linda, this is Trent Archer, Somer's brother and your partner for tomorrow. Trent, this is Linda Wolff, my partner at NYPD."

A firm square hand caught Linda's before she even realized it. "Sorry about the dramatic entrance. Normally that's not my style, but the noisy one there"— he turned his head toward Ali—"is our younger sister, Ali. She doesn't like the bridesmaid's dress and complained about it all the way over here."

"What don't you like about it?" Somer asked,

clearly concerned. "I thought we all agreed on the style." Somer moved Ali away from them and engaged her in heated conversation. Soon the rest of the bridesmaids gathered around them.

"I better see if I can help," Nick said, moving away and leaving Trent and Linda alone.

"So I guess we're walking down the aisle tomorrow," Trent said. He covered the top of Linda's hand with his other and smiled.

"Seems so," Linda replied, returning his smile. "Nick's told me a little about you. You're a cop too."

Trent was nothing like she expected from what Nick had said. Trent was taller than she thought, better built. Somehow the name Trent Archer had conjured up a more casual, preppy, college-campus-police picture than the street-toughened city cops she was used to associating with. Instead Trent was a toned and tapered six-feet tall with a head of hair the color of a field of wheat and eyes the color of dark chocolate. His handshake was firm, hard, and commanding. Maybe being in this wedding wouldn't be a total waste of a few vacation days after all.

"Nick did tell me that his partner was the better-looking one, and now I see that it's true," Trent said.

When his eyes flickered down to her mouth, then back up, Linda suddenly realized how warm and personal the extended handshake had become. She gently eased her hand away and stepped back.

"So do you like the dress?" Trent asked, gesturing

to the circle of women still intently engaged in discussion.

"It's okay."

"You don't sound that excited about it."

"It's a dress for one day. When I get married—if I get married—I'd let my attendants wear jeans and a T-shirt if they wanted to."

Trent laughed. "There is no way that would happen here. I think our mom's been planning this wedding since Somer was six. It's all the bells and whistles for this brouhaha. Our mother is a bit quirky; wait until you meet her. I'll just bet that she has some surprises in store for Somer tomorrow too." He crooked his finger and motioned Linda closer to him. "Stay close," he said lowering his voice to a whisper. "If she unleashes the doves tomorrow, we'll duck under the choir loft so they don't leave any surprises on us."

"Thanks, I will. And I'm glad you made it here tonight. I was about to have to walk through the procedure with one of the altar boys," Linda said. She glanced over at the circle of women still apparently discussing the dress situation. "I forgot that Somer had a younger sister. From the way you two were sparring when you first came in, I thought Ali was your wife."

Trent's laugh came out in a rush of air. "Never. I mean Ali's cute and everything I suppose, but no way would I ever marry a she-devil like that. We Archers are legendary in our bickering. Archer women more so. Nick's going to have his hands full with Somer."

"So you don't like a woman with an opinion then?"

Trent's eyes narrowed. "Well, your name certainly does fit you."

"What do you mean?"

"You pounced on that comment quick enough. Like a wolf on its prey."

Momentarily speechless, Linda watched Trent's gaze follow the blush that she felt inch its way across her cheeks. When his gaze caught her eyes again, he winked, and she felt heat build on her skin. Annoyed with her reaction to him, she flicked her gaze down to his Adam's apple and then away from him entirely until she could think of something sensible to say. When Nick's shrill whistle sliced through the vestibule and echoed in the church beyond, announcing to everyone that it was time to begin, she was never more grateful for the moment.

Father Spencer, church pastor, urged everyone to take a seat so he could fill them in on the service.

"Sorry about the wolf comment," Trent said, sliding into the pew next to Linda.

"It's okay," she returned. "Just get your foot out of your mouth before someone notices." She gave him a "gotcha" wink and turned to listen to the directions.

Trent felt his grin widen in response. He liked this woman, he decided. She had a little fire in her. He leaned back and tried to get as comfortable as possible on the hard wooden seat. In doing so, his knees sprawled wide, one of them a scant inch away from Linda's. He straightened, turned slightly, and hung his wrist on the pew behind her. She glanced at his arm and then at him. *Check*, he thought, equating his move to strategy in a game of chess. He settled into the pew and waited. It was her move.

For the next few minutes, she remained perfectly still as Father Spencer outlined the rituals of the wedding ceremony. Each time she shifted, Trent mirrored her move. They were playing cat and mouse, and he knew she knew it. A few minutes of moves and countermoves later, there came a rescuing rustle of sheet music and a few testing notes from the organ in the choir loft, putting an end to the silent battle they were fighting for the time being.

"The organist is ready," Father Spencer announced.

A hammering of footsteps echoed as everyone got up from their seats in the pews. Father Spencer directed each person into position with the precision of a bandleader, while everyone waited for instructions and cues. Nick and Somer had elected to have the attendants walk down the aisle as pairs, so they lined up in the aisle as couples.

"You were doing that on purpose," Linda whispered to Trent.

"Doing what?" Trent asked, clearly feigning ignorance.

"You didn't have to sit so close with your arm behind me. I'm your partner, not your girlfriend," she answered.

"Don't want one," Trent replied casually.

"Which? Partner or girlfriend?"

"At this point, either," he replied, another grin growing on his lips.

Linda was about to hurl a snappy comeback when Father Spencer appeared right next to them. "We're walking, we're walking," he prompted. Linda had no recourse but to take the elbow Trent had presented to her and walk with him to the front of the church.

His arm pulled her hand against his ribs when they took slow steps forward, being careful not to catch up with the attendants who were in front of them. As her hand rested on the sleeve of his jacket, she felt the warmth of his skin through the fabric, making her much too aware of how solid he felt.

A pleasant scent rose as they walked and drifted through her senses, a scent she couldn't identify. Something pure, not perfumed. One of those natural soaps, maybe. It was nice. Very nice.

And to her surprise he moved with a relaxed poise as he walked. Not the swagger she expected from him, but more like he was strolling in time to the music.

"How am I doing?" he suddenly whispered.

She turned her head. "Not bad. Can you dance too?"

Trent winced. "Hardly."

"Seems like you could."

"Let's see if you still think so after the first dance we have."

They reached the altar rail and followed the instructions given to them at the back of the church, separating and taking their places just across the aisle from each other. Nick came out from the vestibule and Ali, the maid of honor, and the best man soon joined him at the altar.

Turning to face the back, Linda watched as Somer began the long walk with her mother. Though her father would probably be watching from his place in the heavens, Mrs. Archer would be the one to give Somer's hand to Nick.

Just before Somer reached the altar, Linda glanced across at Trent and found his eyes resting steadily on her as if they had been there for some time. He smiled briefly and then looked away and the rest of the instructions began. As Father Spencer spoke about what came next and the nuptial mass, she studied her partner more carefully.

He was casually dressed, like most of the men in the wedding party. His jeans looked new and fit snugly across lean hips. Beneath a lightweight jacket he wore a white button-down shirt. He stood with feet widespread, both hands slipped into his rear pockets. The stance pulled his open jacket aside, hinting at a broad chest and flat stomach.

Father Spencer gestured and Trent's head swiveled to follow the pointing finger. His profile was striking, and Linda wondered why she thought that. At first glance she thought he had the kind of face that would look twenty when he was fifty, but from this angle she could see a combination of features that were both strong and memorable. The golden lights in the old church gilded his sandy hair, which was cut regulation-short but still somehow seemed to invite her touch.

Maybe it was just the moment that made her sweep his bearing and linger a bit longer than necessary on his chest. Or maybe she had given him a twice-over because he seemed different from the men she normally associated with. The rough-and-tumble, hard-drive New York cops rarely gave her another look.

He turned and caught her looking at him. "I knew you liked me," he mouthed. Before she could refute it by looking away, he pointed to Father Spencer and, with an added point for emphasis, suggested by body language that she listen to him.

But instead of being angry, Linda found herself caught up in the expression on his face. The half smile he flashed her transformed it into such a picture of charm that she wondered why he didn't want a girlfriend at this time. Did he get his heart broken recently? Maybe more than once? And while she was gawking, she couldn't help but notice that even from a distance, she could see the most beautiful eyelashes she had ever seem on a man. Dark and thick, they managed to cast a shadow on his cheeks when his lids lowered as he smiled.

She lowered her head and dug the toe of her shoe into the thick carpet. What on earth was she doing thinking about him like that?

Just then Father Spencer's voice rose, "And that will be the cue for the recessional."

The organ boomed and she and Trent met in the center of the aisle. She took his elbow willingly this time and walked to the back of the church.

They ran through the ceremony one more time before the wedding party and guests clustered in the back of the church to get directions to the rehearsal dinner.

"Did you drive here?" Trent asked her suddenly.

Linda nodded.

"Too bad. I thought we could ride over to the restaurant together." He opened the exterior church door and instinctively put a hand to the small of her back to allow her out first. They walked that way down the steps. "If you get there before I do, save me a seat," he said.

She stood there, looking at him, thinking she shouldn't encourage him with a reply, yet answering, "And if you get there first, save a seat for me."

"Deal," he said, waiting until she was in the driver's seat of her car before jogging off toward his.

A warning siren went off inside her head. *Don't be thinking this is anything more than a wedding setup. Sunday you're going back to the city and you're never going to see him again. Remember that. Let well enough alone.*

Chapter Two

The rehearsal dinner was served buffet style in the back room of Magee's, Somer and Nick's favorite restaurant. When Trent arrived, Linda was already there. He picked up a plate and got in line. There were a few people between them, but she wasn't totally out of his sight line so he used the time to study her more carefully than he had at the church.

He wondered what she would look like if her hair weren't pulled back into a ponytail set at the nape of her neck. He remembered that her eyes were blue, unusual for someone with hair the color of midnight, but that made her only more interesting. The sound of her laugh suddenly cut through the air as she reacted to whatever it was one of the other groomsmen had just said to her. He liked her tone; it made him smile along with her. When she turned slightly to re-place a serving spoon in its holder, he took in the gentle curve of her cheek that led to her unpainted mouth. A little lipstick would make her lips look fuller. He did like a woman with full lips.

From living with three women most of his male life, he recognized the navy suit she wore as top quality, probably a designer brand. But it was cut a little boxy and hid the shape of her body. Being a New York City cop, she was probably athletic and therefore lean and toned, but she had piqued his curiosity and now he wanted to know for sure. Maybe the bridesmaid's dress she'd wear the next day would give him a better idea. When she stepped back to allow Nick to snatch a dinner roll from the buffet table, Trent followed the curve of her calf to sensible brown shoes. Pity, he thought. From what he could see, she had the promise of great legs. A pair of heels would really set them off.

From the short time he had spent with her at the church, he sensed that she was a bit reserved, but her interaction with him hinted of a more playful side. Now that he had paid more attention to the packaging, he decided having to pair up with her for most of the day tomorrow probably would give him more of a chance to find out.

He saw her pick up a bottle of water and head for the long dining table. He finished filling his plate and followed her, waiting until she sat down before swinging his leg over the seat of the chair next to her as if he were climbing over a fence and depositing his plate on the table. There was enough food on it to feed about three people.

Linda looked at it and then at him. "I think you should have asked for a platter."

"Think so?" he asked, pushing some of the roast beef back before it slid onto the tablecloth. He looked at the sensible combination on her plate. "On a diet?"

"No," she replied quickly. "I like to eat right and stay in shape."

He almost told her that he'd like to see what kind of shape that was, but decided against it. He didn't want to seem too pushy. "For your job on the force," he finally said.

She nodded as she pushed a celery stick around some salad dressing. "It gets dicey sometimes, on the street. You have to be ready to go."

"How long have you been a cop?"

"Almost seven years."

"That means you're . . ." He raised his chin doing some mental calculations. "Somewhere in your thirties."

"Dangerous to ask a woman her age," Linda warned and then said, "Thirty-five, actually."

"Maybe dangerous to admit it so fast," Trent quipped. "You look younger."

"Are you trying to flirt with me?" she suddenly asked.

"No, just issuing a compliment." He lifted his glass and took two quick swallows before running his thumb along the corner of his mouth, all without taking his gaze from her face.

"So how old are you?" she asked.

"Thirty," Trent replied. He held up his hand. "I know. I look older."

"Younger, actually," Linda said, beginning to eat.

Trent drew back. "Well, now I'd say you're flirting with me."

Linda laughed. "If I was flirting, you'd know it."

"Then I'll be careful to look for signs over the next day or so," he said confidently before filling his mouth with some potato salad. He studied Linda for a minute as he swallowed it. "And if I miss it, feel free to tell me," he added.

"Isn't there a girlfriend to anger if I do that?"

"There's a girl friend, but she isn't coming to the wedding."

Linda looked puzzled. "Your sister didn't invite your girlfriend to the wedding?"

"Girl *friend*," Trent corrected, carefully separating the words, "as in a friend who just happens to be a girl. It isn't anything serious. I thought that if I did bring her . . ." Trent's mind went on rapid-fire imaging thinking about just what would happen if he brought any girl to the wedding. His mom would be ecstatic thinking he was next to get married. Ali would think he fell victim to Grandmother's sapphire ring and would spend the day getting even with him. He forced himself out of the deep reverie. No sense trying to explain the newly is-sued Archer family curse to Linda. "Ah, never mind. Let's just say she was busy this weekend. What about you? Any takers on the NYPD?"

"I don't date cops," Linda replied quickly.

"Why not?"

"Too complicated."

"For?" Trent dragged out the word.

Linda shrugged. "You know. You're a cop."

He pressed his shoulders against the chair back and assessed the subject of the discussion for a mo-ment, then shook his head. "I have absolutely no idea what you're talking about."

Linda put her fork down and turned more fully to him. "It's like . . . well, it seems that every time I thought it would be okay to date any of the guys at the precinct, dates would turn into some kind of competi-tion." She threw up a hand. "Like we were still at the academy and I wasn't allowed to get a higher test score or do more push-ups or else I'd hurt their male pride."

"Because you are a woman?"

"Because I'm a female cop."

Trent made a disdainful sound before speaking. "I thought most men were beyond that these days. Maybe you were reading too much into it."

She shook her head. "I don't think so." She began to say more but then changed her mind. It wasn't the only reason she wouldn't date a police officer, but it was good enough for now. "Let's just say there weren't many second dates," she added.

"You're kidding? A woman with your"—his gaze flickered downward before starting up again—"face."

"So you're a body man then?" There was coolness to her voice, as though the tone would put him in his place.

He was not going to allow it. "Yes, ma'am. I like the curves and angles. In fact I'd like to—"

Linda raised her hand to stop him. "Spare me the graphic details, please."

A broad grin spread across Trent's face. "It's motorcycles. You didn't let me finish. After I retire from the force I'd like to open up a shop and build custom motorcycles. I like the way you can disguise the gas tank to look like something else and angle the exhaust to accent the wheels. From the day I borrowed a friend's old rebuilt Harley and took it out on the interstate, motorcycles fascinated me."

Linda tipped her head aslant. This was the second time today she had walked into his trap. "Do you always set up people like that?"

She saw a wicked gleam light his eyes. "You make it so easy that I can't help myself," he answered, smiling. When she didn't smile back at him, his smile faded. "But I meant it in the nicest possible way, of course."

"Of course," she replied, getting up and heading for the dessert table.

Trent followed close behind her. "So what do you do for fun after a shift on the mean streets of New York?" he asked, picking up a plate with a slice of cheesecake on it.

Linda watched him add some brownies to it. "You must have really paid attention at the academy. They teach you never to give up once you have a goal in mind."

"And what goal would that be?"

"Could be one of two," Linda replied, heading back to the table with her choice. "Either to find out everything you can about me or to annoy me no end." When Trent sat down next to her again, he gave her a lopsided grin that, despite her attempt to keep it casual, set her heart pounding for some reason.

"The instructors taught us not to rule out any possibilities, so the goals you listed could actually be one and the same," he warned.

"I suppose you also graduated at the head of the class."

"Nah, not this guy. The fieldwork came easy, but the book stuff, not so much. I had to work hard to stay in the middle. A lot of the guys had sponsors of a sort; someone who helped them get into police work and then into the academy. I'd like to think I did it all on my own."

Linda quirked her lips. "The independent kind."

"I like to think so."

"In my experience, I find that independent people

tend to put other people off," Linda replied without hesitating.

Trent shrugged. "I find that people seem to like me just the way I am."

"It's pretty unusual for a police officer to notice what other people think of him."

"Why?"

"It just *is*," Linda said with emphasis on the last word.

Trent cocked his head trying to read the reason behind her statement. She looked so serious, her eyes suddenly darker than the bright blue they were, the change in color brought on by the undeniable emotion he could see darting there. He suddenly wanted to make her laugh.

"Well, people like me because, hey, let's face it, how could anyone resist my considerable charms? I'm successful, handsome as all get out, and intelligent and"—he winked—"available."

Linda stared at him before bursting out laughing. "You need to add impossible to that list." Then she stood up and headed for the door.

"Go ahead and run," Trent called out after her. "It won't do you any good. You're stuck with me for the whole day tomorrow."

Trent chuckled as she paused briefly at the door to roll her eyes at him before leaving.

"Good," Ali said, coming up from behind him on her way to dessert. "You scared off another one."

Trent nodded. "One less to have to worry about if that ring voodoo is going to work."

Now it was Ali's turn to roll her eyes. "She seems too smart for that."

"Probably," Trent agreed as his sister continued on her quest for sweets.

He leaned back in his chair and toyed with the idea of going out to see if Linda had left the parking lot yet. No, he decided, there was no real reason for him to do that. He'd let her go. This time. Tomorrow was another story. They would be virtually united at the hip from the ceremony to well into the reception.

And he had to admit, it wouldn't be all that bad. They made a pretty nice-looking couple. She was pretty; had the potential to be beautiful with a little makeup. And he'd bet next week's pay she was going to look great in her bridesmaid's gown.

But there was more to her than just the physical. His initial assessment of her was correct, and, despite her attempt not to give him too much information, he had found out just enough to pique his curiosity. Now he wanted to know more. As he thought about that for a moment, he had to admit that, standing next to her, it wouldn't be all that difficult for him to smile for all those pictures that would be taken tomorrow.

He only hoped that no one else in his family was going to notice.

Chapter Three

The bridesmaids all met at the World of Hair Studio to have their hair done the next day. Linda sat in the chair and tried to relax. She hated having her hair done. A ponytail or clip at the nape of her neck was good enough for her. Now a stylist about ten years younger than her pulled, poked, and prodded her hair into a sweep of curls that fell gracefully over her shoulders. A circle of fresh flowers would eventually replace the stiff blue police cap she normally wore.

Her minded wandered as the stylist tried to coax an errant curl into place. *Trent Archer*, she thought staring at her reflection in the mirror. *You're going to see him again today. You're going to have to walk down the aisle with him, stand for a thousand pictures with him, and dance with him.*

The stylist caught her smiling. "Like the style?"

"It's fine," Linda replied. But her hairstyle wasn't what had made her smile. Trent had professed that he was no dancer. That very well may be, but he was a smooth mover. In more ways than one, she suspected. She looked forward to shutting him down.

"All done," she heard the stylist say.

When she looked at the finished product in the mirror, she had to admit, it was a very flattering hairstyle. Her dark hair framed her face in curls Linda didn't think she could ever have evoked on her own. They seemed to call attention to her eyes and make them bluer. She wondered briefly if Trent would like the way she looked before chiding herself for caring what he thought. It wasn't like her to worry about things like that.

So why couldn't she seem to get the idea completely out of her mind?

Somer was the last to be finished and Linda had to admit, Somer was the most beautiful bride she had even seen. And Nick was head over heels in love with her. They were the perfect couple beginning a promising perfect life together today.

As Linda watched the bridal party deal out the oohs and ahs, a pang of emotion she couldn't quite comprehend settled in her chest. Regret? Envy? Melancholy? No, not any of those. There was no room for them on a day like today. But she had felt something, something else, something not entirely familiar to her.

Somer came up to her, hands extended. "Linda, you look beautiful."

"Not compared to you." Linda pressed a quick kiss to Somer's cheek. "You look perfect."

"I feel perfect," Somer replied, smiling.

"You and Nick are going to have the most wonderful life together," Linda said. "I can feel it."

Somer nodded. "I feel it too." She turned to the bridal party. "The limo is here to take us to my house." She angled the watch on her wrist to her eyes. "The makeup artist should be there already." She clapped her hands together. "Let's go get beautified, get dressed, and get this show on the road before Nick changes his mind!"

Amid laughs, everyone walked to the waiting white stretch limo. As Linda waited her turn to get into the car, another pang of emotion tightened her chest. She might very well get "beautified" as Somer suggested, but with no one special to notice, it would all go to waste once she got back to the city.

Somer was incredibly lucky to have found someone who loved her and accepted her for what she was. Linda had given up on that a long time ago.

A few hours later Linda walked up the steps of the church. At the door, she felt a rush of anticipation. Trent Archer was probably inside already. She could very well run in to him in the vestibule.

She paused before going in and wondered what he

would think when he saw her. Her hair was perfect and her makeup was perfect. Maybe today even she was perfect.

She took a deep breath and stepped inside. Disappointment welled inside her when she didn't see Trent.

The bridesmaids were ushered to a room right off the vestibule. Tess, Somer's mother, was already waiting for them inside.

After greeting both her daughters, Tess walked to Linda and gave her a hug. "Linda, you look lovely."

"Thank you, Mrs. Archer," Linda replied. "I'm sorry I haven't had much time to talk to you. Nick speaks very highly of you."

Tess smiled. "He's a wonderful man. I know he'll make Somer very happy. And we can get to know each other better on Sunday at the brunch we're having for everyone at my house. You are coming, aren't you?"

"I wouldn't miss it, ma'am."

"Call me Tess. Nick has told me so much about you that I feel I already know you."

Linda nodded. "Tess, then."

"I appreciate that you took some time off to be in the wedding party. Your being here is very important to Nick."

"I wouldn't have missed his wedding for anything," Linda replied, smiling.

Somer seemed to be having trouble with her veil

and Tess rushed to help her, leaving Linda alone. While Ali, as the maid of honor, assumed her role as controller of the wedding day necessities, Linda stepped in front of one of the mirrors that had been brought in for the day. She looked at herself from head to toe for the first time since she put on her dress.

The strapless satin A-line dress with trumpet skirt designed by Vera Wang seemed foreign to her. She was more at ease in classic separates made by a more affordable designer. She didn't particualry care for the color, a dark tan that reminded her of a good latte. Around her waist a dark brown sash with a large half bow in the back did contrast nicely, however. The bow came up to the middle of her back and was pinned with an ornate brooch that would be one of the first things to go once she got the dress off after the day was over.

One of the other bridesmaids stood next to her for a few seconds and Linda realized how white her bare shoulders looked next to the other attendant's. She should have gone to a tanning salon, she decided. All of the other bridesmaids seemed to have had a session or two under the lights. She would rather sit out in the sun doing paperwork or reports rather than bake in an ultraviolet oven. But it was only May with not enough warm sun yet to put some color in her skin.

She shook her head. Great, she thought, the guests

would probably wonder if she had just recovered from a serious illness or wonder if she was an albino. That's how pale she looked. She'd blame the dress color on that when everyone gathered to look at the wedding pictures in a few months.

"Five minutes," someone shouted and a buzz of excitement rose, sounding like a swarm of bees as the bridesmaids made their last-minute adjustments to hair and makeup.

Linda turned to walk back into the church proper to take her place in line when she saw Trent. He stood just outside the vestibule, his eyes slowly scanning the area. He honed in on her as surely as she did him, his gaze going no farther once it found her.

Something tight gripped her chest as she inhaled sharply with the contact of his intent look. Her heart slammed against her chest when she saw his smile begin. His gaze swept to her feet and then up again to her eyes. When he caught her gaze again, his smile exploded, and along with it, the breath she had been holding.

He walked to her, hands extended, palms up. "You look beautiful."

She gripped the bouquet she held tightly with one hand while giving him the other. He took her hand firmly and pulled her gently forward, kissing her on the cheek. His lips were warm, his breath moist as his lips lingered a bit longer than was necessary for a polite greeting. By the time he pulled back, she knew she must be the color of the assortment of the pink and crimson flowers in her hand.

"Thank you," she somehow managed to say. She braved a hurried sweeping glance of him. "And you look nice too." A telltale waver was in her voice.

"Just nice?" He stepped back and turned in a circle as if to give her a better look.

"Very nice?" Linda replied.

"I'd say rather handsome."

"Very nice *and* modest," she returned.

Just then the double doors opened and organ music rumbled overhead. The church fell silent except for a few secret whispers as the guests rose and turned to get a glimpse of the wedding party.

The first strains of the "Wedding March" began and Trent reached for her elbow, urging her into line behind the lead couples. Once in place, she tucked her hand into the fold of his arm, finding a warmth there that soothed her nerves.

"Here we go," he whispered to her as Ali and the best man got in line behind them but in front of the flower girl and ring bearer.

As the couples began their walk down the aisle one by one, she heard him count off, timing their own entrance the way the priest had asked them to do at the rehearsal. She felt the muscles of his arm tense and angled her head toward him.

"Three, four, and one two . . ."

He was still counting, oblivious to anything else. She almost laughed out loud. Just before it was their turn to step onto the white runner, she saw him suck in his stomach and press his shoulders back.

"Showtime," he said, covering her fingers on his arm for just a second before starting the walk with her toward the altar.

As she slowly walked down the aisle on his arm, she was conscious of the scent of incense, the faint smell of candlewick, and the sweet aroma rising from the mass of flowers in the church. Though her common sense told her not to do it, she cut her gaze toward Trent. And that was the exact moment it happened.

Something jolted inside her, something strong and compelling telling her that this day was going to change her in ways she hadn't expected. It was the excitement of the day, the celebration, the anticipation, she reasoned, trying to shake off the feeling. But it stayed strong and sharp on the fringes of her mind no matter how sensible she tried to be.

Chasing the warning to the back of her mind, she took her place at the altar and, for the next hour, concentrated on the marriage of two people perfect for each other. The soft-spoken responses, the exchange of vows between bride and groom spiraled around her, and she wondered briefly if she would ever find someone to share something as wonderful as this day.

The priest paused just before the final pronouncement and asked the married couples in attendance to celebrate the marriage of Somer and Nick by silently renewing their own vows.

For Linda, there was no spouse with whom to reaffirm promises, no significant other, not even someone she saw casually. She looked down at her bouquet, feeling vulnerable and conspicuous. When she looked back up, she found Trent looking at her and their gazes locked and held.

They didn't smile, didn't otherwise acknowledge each other, but she could feel the fascination she had for him grow as the priest continued with the ceremony and sealed the marriage compact.

"I now pronounce you husband and wife. You may now kiss the bride," she heard the priest say, and only then did she break contact with Trent's gaze to join in the thunderous applause that rolled through the church.

The photos at the altar were done and the wedding party prepared to exit the church and take on the waiting well-wishers. Two by two the attendants walked down the brick church steps dodging a shower of flower petals and birdseed mixed with bubbles blown by some guests before they slipped into a waiting stretch limousine that would take them to the reception. The wedding party shared the black stretch limousine while the flower girl, ring bearer, best man, maid of honor, and bride and groom rode in the pure-white stretch.

On the way, organized confusion reigned in the car as one of the groomsmen popped the cork on a bottle of champagne and doled it out. The bubbles tickled Linda's nose as she sipped it and she hiccupped, producing laughter from the rest of the party.

"Better not let her have too much," the grooms-man said to Trent, "or you'll have to dance with someone else."

"Got it under control," Trent replied, taking the glass from Linda's hand. "Ginger ale only for you," he said to Linda.

Linda snatched the fluted glass back from him. "I'm quite capable of deciding that I can have one celebratory glass of champagne," she fired back, draining the small amount left in the glass in one gulp.

"Since you just had one, you'll be having two then, counting the toast," one of the bridesmaids reminded her.

"Yes, two," Linda agreed handing the empty glass back to Trent. "Or three if I so choose," she added, eyes locked with his.

Trent's eyes danced mischievously. "Or more if you'd like."

"Whoa, Trent," one of the groomsmen said. "Slow down, you just met the lady a few days ago."

"Did that ever stop him?" another asked.

Linda felt her jaw drop open. She looked at Trent

who just winked in return. The action produced hearty laughs from those watching while Trent acknowledged them while raising his hands in mock victory. He turned back to her and she forced herself to turn her head away to stare out the car window when his eyes settled on her lips. She rode the rest of the way in silence while the others finished one bottle of champagne and opened another.

They arrived at the banquet hall and the photographer directed them to the manicured grounds for more pictures. Somer and Nick did the traditional pictures with family, with the flower girl and ring bearer, with Ali as maid of honor and the best man, and the sequence of shots seemed to go on forever.

When it came time for pictures of the bride and her bridesmaids, Trent didn't even bother to disguise his obvious interest in the shots. He sat on a low retaining wall watching the session intently, concentrating his gaze on Linda more than on his sisters.

"Let's get everyone back together," the photographer finally said. "Pair up, please."

Trent took his place next to Linda and they found themselves nudged, pulled, and coaxed into positions that satisfied the photographer's trained eye. After a flurry of movements, Linda found herself standing alone next to Trent while they waited for the photographer to set up the next shot.

"I'm sorry, Linda," Trent said as the other attendants were instructed to line up next to them. "I had no right poking fun at you like that while we were in the limo."

"Move closer together," the photographer said, motioning with one hand and holding his camera firmly in the other.

She felt Trent move closer and for some reason her heart flailed like a wounded bird. "You're right, you didn't," she whispered back at him.

"I guess I was showing off a little."

Linda huffed. "Why do boys always seem to do that?"

"Boys? I stopped being a boy about ten years ago."

Linda glanced over her shoulder at him. "Really now?"

"You two, on the end," the photographer said, "Look here, please."

Trent and Linda stilled at the command. They followed the photographer's ensuing instructions, presenting first left shoulders to the viewfinder, then right shoulders. As the photographer snapped pictures from various angles, to Linda's surprise Trent not only spanned her hipbones with his hands, but he pulled her back until she nestled snugly against his hip. He was the perfect height for her and she seemed to fit as though they had been made for each other.

The closeness brought her into the realm of his aftershave, a totally rich and very masculine scent she hadn't smelled before, but one she would definitely remember. While they stood immobile that way for a while as the pictures were being snapped, she felt him settle against her and thought she heard him swallow as though he was holding something back.

"Now we'll do couples," the photographer said. Everyone backed off into pairs and waited their turn.

"I know why I'm in the wedding party," Trent said once the pictures of Ali and the best man began, "but why did you agree to it?"

"I got Nick as a partner right out of the academy and I've been his partner ever since. I'd do anything for him." She ran her hand down her organza skirt. "Even wear this."

Nick laughed. "It's not so bad."

"It's annoying."

He put his finger between the stiff collar of his tuxedo shirt and his neck. "So's this. But I feel the same way about my sister like you do about Nick. I'd do anything for her." He glanced at Somer, contently wrapped in Nick's arms and watching the photo shoot. "I've never seen her more beautiful."

Linda kept her face forward pretending to be interested in the shots so she wouldn't have to confront his eyes. "They say all brides are beautiful."

"And so are their bridesmaids," Nick whispered into her ear.

Linda gripped her bouquet with both hands. She had no response for him.

The photographer led them to a tree and instructed Trent to stand as close to the trunk as he could. Then he directed Linda to stand in front of Trent. He raised the camera. "Put your arms around her, put your hands on her forearms and pull her into your hip."

Trent hesitated a little and then complied. "Like this?" he asked, trying to interpret what the photographer wanted.

Linda tried her best to relax as Trent's arms encircled her. When he pulled her back against his hip she heard him grunt.

"Straighten up and try to relax," the photographer said to him.

Trent shifted. "The pin on the bow in the back of her dress is poking me in the side."

The photographer lowered his camera. "Try to find a position that's more comfortable for you. The discomfort is showing on your face."

Linda moved away while Trent adjusted his position. Satisfied, he straightened his shoulders and pulled her back to him. "Why in the world is a tiny pin like that so bothersome?" he asked, trying to find a better angle.

"I don't know," Linda replied. "Can we just take the picture and be done with it?"

About that time Trent's eyes widened. "Wait a minute," he said, holding her out at an arm's length and looking directly at the big, brown half-bow set vertically at the back of her dress. "It's not the pin that's the problem, is it?" He spun her around. "That bow is large enough to for you to . . ." He spun her back and looked into her eyes. "You're carrying, aren't you?"

Linda tossed her head and tried not to look nervous. "I don't know what you mean." Trent pulled her toward him and she had no recourse but to hold her bouquet in one hand and put the other on his chest.

He leaned forward and whispered. "You're wearing your gun to my sister's wedding."

"You're a police officer. You know we're supposed to carry our weapons at all times, even off duty, she whispered back.

"This is a wedding, my sister's wedding. Just because it's in New Jersey it doesn't mean that Tony Soprano is coming."

"What's the problem?" the photographer called out.

Trent waved to him. "Just a minute."

Linda felt the heat rise on her chest. "Habit, I guess. I'm sorry."

"You should be."

"Are you going to rat me out?" she asked.

"No, but right after this you're going to go to the manager's office, take off the gun, and have him lock it in the safe until after the reception."

Linda nodded. "It was a dumb thing for me to do. I owe you. Just don't make a scene. Please."

"Can we get on with the pictures?" the photographer said. "We have a lot more to take."

"Take this one first," Trent said right before he put

his hand on the back of Linda's head, pulling her forward before kissing her hard.

"There," he said when he released her. "Consider the debt paid."

Chapter Four

"**U**narmed?"

"Yes." Linda hoped the sound of her voice and look on her face said annoyed, although embarrassed was probably more like it. She felt his hand on the small of her back as though he wanted to be sure. "The gun is in the safe in the manager's office," she said stepping away. "There's no need to check. I do keep my word."

"Good because we're about to make a grand entrance and I don't think you should do it guns blazing."

About that time some of the guests noticed the arrival of the bridal party. They lined the pathway leading to the reception hall applauding as the bridal party made their way inside. From the outside it looked like a historic Victorian house, but the inside had been renovated to accommodate weddings and other large affairs.

An elegant staircase curved up to smaller rooms from the entry hall and wide double doors were rolled back to combine two bottom floor rooms into one large area. The oak floors were polished to perfection and the ceiling-to-floor windows were decorated with sheer curtains to allow the light to stream through.

The introduction of the wedding party began. As Linda and Trent inched forward, a pang of guilt struck her. "I am sorry, you know," she whispered. "I shouldn't have brought that."

"Uh-huh." Trent agreed taking a step forward.

"And you shouldn't have kissed me."

"Uh-huh."

She swung her head toward his. "That's all you're going to say?"

"For now. We're on."

". . . put your hands together for bridesmaid Linda Wolff, accompanied by the brother of the bride, Trent Archer."

They walked in precision to the center of the floor where two other couples waited. After introducing the flower girl, ring bearer, maid of honor, and best man, the announcer called, "And now I give you Mr. and Mrs. Nicholas Daultry."

Trent burst into applause before putting two fingers

in his mouth and producing an earsplitting whistle. Linda clapped and stepped back to get out of the direct fire of the blast.

"Now you're stuck with her," Trent called out to Nick as he passed.

Across the dance floor the DJ turned up the music and said into his mike, "Now Nick and Somer will dance the first dance to their favorite song, 'Suddenly' by Billy Ocean."

Linda watched as Nick captured Somer in his arms and dipped his head to kiss her before spinning with her into the center of the dance floor. Somer rested her hands on Nick's chest and let him lead her in a slow rock to the music. The photographer circled around them snapping one shot after another, but they seemed oblivious to anything but each other. Linda felt her heart catch and wondered if she would ever find someone that could make the world melt away as Nick seemed to have done for Somer.

After a few minutes, Trent postured an exaggerated bow. "Shall we join them, Ms. Wolff?"

Linda gave her head a tiny shake. She hadn't noticed that the other couples were already dancing. Before she had a chance to react, he took her bouquet and handed it to the woman closest to him and then captured her hand. He swooped her into his arms and snuggled her close, resting his jaw against her cheek.

Linda felt an awkward thrill of intimacy with his action and it sent a shiver through her. He hadn't done anything but free her of the bouquet so they could dance, but she liked the way he'd done it— without asking, without fumbling for a place to put it. She smiled, knowing he wouldn't see it, and enjoyed the dance.

He didn't have the grace of some of the other men she'd danced with over the years. Instead he seemed content to just nestle her against him and circle the floor with small steps. With his face so close to hers, she could feel a faint scratching from facial hair already growing after his morning shave. She could smell a stronger aroma of his cologne, a distinct blend of herb, citrus, and musk.

His hand was wide and covered hers completely. The muscles beneath her hand on his chest felt hard and toned even through the coarse fabric of his tuxedo. She fought the urge to move her hand around his neck so she could feel the hair just above his collar curl around her fingers. She'd been wondering since she saw him if it felt as soft as it looked.

But she balked and stayed content to dance in his arms. There she concentrated on getting to know the other textures and scents that made up Trent Archer. As the dance continued, she came to realize that Trent fascinated her much more than he should considering she'd only met him the day before.

"You dance wonderfully," she said to pull her attention away from the way she seemed to fit him perfectly.

He backed away a bit and looked into her eyes. "Really? You aren't just being kind, are you?"

Her heart fluttered. "No, I'm not the being-kind type."

Trent's hand moved to the hollow of her back and he continued to look into her eyes. "What type are you?"

"I thought we did this already."

"Not totally."

"Why do you want to know?"

He brought her back up against his body. "Because I do." He tried to make two quick spins with her in his arms and nearly lost his balance. "Sorry," he said, realizing he nearly sent them tumbling to the floor. "Fred Astaire I'm not."

She laughed. "You were doing fine before you started to show off. I don't need someone who wants to try out for one of the dance shows, I only need . . ."

"You," he finished for her. "Meaning me."

The song ended and everyone began clapping, giving Linda no room to counter Trent's claim. Then they walked from the dance floor to the head table. Trent stepped behind Linda's chair and pulled it out for her. As he moved to his chair, someone handed Linda back her bouquet and she plopped it down with a heavy thump at the edge of the table between two white candles, as they had been instructed to do.

As soon as Trent was seated he turned his full attention to her. "What made you so testy all of a sudden?"

they really did both love the bride and groom, how they both would rather be watching Game Six of the Stanley Cup playoffs at that moment.

"Will you be coming to the brunch tomorrow?" Trent asked her.

"For a few minutes," Linda replied. "I have to be on duty bright and early on Monday, and I would like some time to unwind." She looked up into his direct gaze. He did have some devastatingly gorgeous eyes.

"Coffee?" a server asked.

"Yes, please," Linda said jumping at the chance to look away from him.

"Linda?"

The tone of his voice compelled her to look into his eyes again. "Yes?"

"Are you afraid of me?"

"No." The word came out more like a stutter than a denial. "Why do you ask?"

"Because your hand is shaking." He touched the knuckle of her index finger where it wrapped around the handle of the cup. At the contact she jerked back and nearly spilled the coffee.

"Excitement. Nerves maybe," she said setting the cup back into the saucer on the table. "Certainly not fear." She looked out into the crowd hoping to find some concrete thought to put between her and one very attractive man from New Jersey who had sent her senses all out of whack. "Excitement. That's it. Aren't you excited?"

"I don't need anyone, let alone an accomplished flirt from New Jersey who kisses women without asking them first."

"You're angry about the comment I made on the dance floor and the fact that I was flirting with you?"

"Yes, among other things."

"And you're angry that I didn't ask you if I could kiss you."

"Yes."

"Would you have let me?"

She pressed her lips together smothering the answer she really wanted to give. "No," she finally said.

"That's why I didn't ask," he reasoned.

She glared at him.

"Okay then, I'm sorry. I didn't know New York City cops were so touchy."

"The fact that I'm a New York City cop doesn't automatically make me touchy."

"Then why are your eyebrows drawn together like that? Keep it up and in a few years you're going to need a Botox shot between your eyes."

She pushed out a long breath of air and forced herself to relax. "Look, I'm just not used to someone flirting with me, that's all."

"You should be." When she turned her head away from him and refused to comment, he continued, "You are a very attractive woman."

She snapped her head back. "And you're a very impossible man."

"And you're almost smiling."

She let out a rush of air. There was no sense sparring with him. She wasn't going to win. Not today. Not at his sister's wedding. Her grin broke at the same time a waitress reached around them and offered to fill their glasses with champagne. Trent nodded his agreement, as did Linda.

Trent leaned over to her. "We'll try breaking you in slowly to the flirting thing again later. Right after the best man's toast, it's my turn." He then turned his attention to the best man who had risen and raised his hands to stop the buzz of conversation in the room. He lifted his glass in response to what the best man was saying and then drank in tribute to his sister and her new husband.

"I believe Somer's brother would like to say a few words," the best man cued.

Trent rose and lifted his glass. "Sis, it goes without saying that I'm happy for you and Nick. I know you'll be happy together for the rest of your lives." He then angled the glass toward his family's table. "Mom, I know you've been dreaming of Somer's wedding almost since the day she was born, so enjoy it." He then looked at his younger sister, Ali. "Mooch, it's you and me against the rings now."

Ali lifted her glass in a return salute.

Trent then turned his attention back to Nick and Somer. "It comes from the bottom of my heart when I say that I know you were made for each other and

deserve a lifetime filled with the love th feeling today." He lifted his glass higher. "T ter and her husband." He drank and then set down on the table. He left his place next to Lii moved to the bridal couple amid cheers and plause of approval. Somer got to her feet a two siblings wrapped their arms around each Trent whispered something into Somer's ear and they looked at each other again, Linda thought saw something deeply emotional glint in both p of eyes.

Nick offered his hand to Trent and he shook wholeheartedly. "Be good to her," Linda heard Tre say, "I love her."

"So do I," Nick answered.

Trent nodded, released Nick's hand, and returned to his chair beside Linda. The waitress refilled his glass and he lifted it toward her. Linda watched the rim of his glass tip up and held his gaze until she thought she could see the sparkle of the bubbles in their dark brown depths. As she watched him finish his champagne, she felt an appreciative warmth flood through her. Trent was a man who was not afraid to show emotion or voice it. How unusual for a cop, for any man for that matter.

Dinner was served and while they ate the prime rib with fresh asparagus and a perfectly baked potato, they talked about safe subjects like his interest in motorcycles, the rising price of gas, and that although

"Absolutely," he said softly. "So much so that I'm going to make sure you have fun today." He got to his feet and pulled her chair back. "May I have this dance, Ms. Wolff?"

He captured her hand and towed her toward the dance floor before she had a chance to refuse.

Chapter Five

A fast song came on next and Trent gyrated his hips and rocked his shoulders, giving dancing his best shot.

Dragging her partner by the hand, Ali danced over to him. "And exactly what style is that you're doing?" she asked, her own dance movements in perfect time to the beat.

"Something never before see by human eyes," Trent replied, breaking into what would be considered a bad dance student's version of tapping while around him the other people on the dance floor laughed in response.

"And may we never see it again," Ali concluded. She tapped Linda on the shoulder. "You should run while you have the chance. He could stomp you to death before the song is over," she said dancing away from them.

Trent looked at Linda's face and saw bemusement. "It's the way we Archers love one another," he explained. "Loud and sarcastic. But just try to be malicious or hurt any of us and we come together like a mountain range. Strong, solid, and impenetrable. No one gets in and no one gets out."

"I kind of thought so," Linda replied.

The next several songs were also fast ones and Trent and Linda decided to keep dancing. As the first notes of the "Macarena" began Trent removed his tuxedo jacket, hung it on the back of the closest chair, and got into line next to Linda. He'd never done this particular line dance before but it was popular in the repertoire of most DJs so he thought he'd give it a try.

"Are you sure you want to do this?" Linda asked as she placed first her right hand behind her head and then her left, sequencing the steps to the dance.

Trent tried to follow her movements. She was already two steps ahead of him. "It may take me a while, but I'll catch on." He did his best to keep pace with her.

Linda placed her hands on her backside and did a slow rock of her hips. "This is where we turn to the right."

She did. He didn't. Trent found himself face-to-face with his mother who was dancing in a line behind him. "Hi, Ma."

"I knew I should have made you go to ballet classes with Ali," Tess Archer teased, circling her finger in the air to get him to turn around and face the opposite direction.

Trent lifted his chin and laughed at the ceiling. "I don't think it would have helped." He hopped ninety degrees and found that he was now two sets behind. Linda had almost turned a full circle. He positioned himself beside her again. "I think I'm getting the hang of this."

She looked down at his feet. They were moving when they should have been still and were still when they should have been moving. "Not quite."

"I give up," he said, breaking into his own version of the dance. "It can't last forever."

It didn't. The next song slowed and Trent held out his arms to Linda, inviting her to continue dancing. She moved into them in one fluid step.

The back of his vest was made of silk, making it easy for her to feel his muscles beneath her hand. She couldn't resist exploring his shoulder blades and the hollow between them. In response his arm tightened around her waist, nestling her securely into the planes of his body. He dropped his head until his lips rested just beside her right ear.

"Whatever you're wearing smells great," he said. "Clean, not heavy like some of the perfumes here tonight."

"It's Amazing Grace."

"Interesting name for a perfume."

"It isn't a perfume exactly. It's more like a total body experience from the bath gel to the lotion to the body spritz. It's meant to be unforgettable."

"Then it's perfect for today because I've been having some sort of total experience since I met you. One I'm not likely to forget for a while, if ever."

"It's been an experience for sure." Linda laughed not knowing if it was out of nervousness at what he said or simply because she felt the same way. Trent's firm chest lifted and fell against hers as an answering chuckle rumbled up from within it.

For the rest of the song, Linda quieted, her thoughts filled with Trent. She really hadn't wanted to be in Nick and Somer's wedding, but partnering with Trent had made it enjoyable. She smiled. *Enjoyable* was a word she normally would not have used in the same sentence as having to wear a bridesmaid's gown all day, but today they seemed to fit together quite nicely.

It seemed a long time since she had laughed so much or talked so freely. Being on the police force in the city meant always keeping your guard up, but today she found that she'd let Trent inside just a little and it appeared he had no intentions of leaving anytime soon. That was okay, she decided. For now.

Nick cut in and exchanged partners with Trent, dancing away with Linda and leaving Somer paired with her brother.

"How are you and Nick's partner getting along?" Somer asked.

Trent shrugged. "She's nice."

"Only nice? You haven't left her side much. Aren't you afraid Mom might notice?"

"I paid a few people to keep Mom busy so she couldn't," Trent said with a grin.

"You did not."

His grin broke into a wide smile. "No, but I probably should have. Since you succumbed to the ring hex, Ali and I have to be vigilant and duck and cover if we see Cupid's arrow coming at us."

"It wasn't Grandma Vicky's ring that made me fall in love with Nick," Somer assured. "It was just coincidence that Mom gave us each one and then I met him."

"So you say. Mom and Grandma Vicky were always close. Who knows what they cooked up?"

"I promise you that last time I was in Mom's basement I checked for cauldrons and there weren't any. Nick came into my life at the perfect time." Somer looked at him dancing with Linda across the room. "And he's the perfect man."

"What am I? Chopped liver?"

"Brothers are not allowed in the comparison tables. But I will ask Linda what she thinks about you if you'd like."

Trent nearly agreed to let her but stopped himself just short. "Don't bother. I already know the answer."

He lifted his chin and gave his head a little shake. "I'm a god."

"That's my brother!" Somer said laughing.

Nick came back with Linda. "I believe I'd like to dance with my wife again," he said, releasing Linda. "Thanks for the dance, Linda."

"My pleasure, Nick."

Nick took Somer's hand and twirled her twice before winding her back into his arms. She laughed when she hit Nick's chest. He dropped his chin and kissed her before taking her back onto the dance floor.

"That's one happy couple," Trent said, watching them dance away.

"They sure are," Linda agreed, her voice a whisper. She watched another couple join Nick and Somer. The four of them now danced arm in arm and she felt a brief pang hit her heart. Maybe there was still time to find someone who could make her feel the way Somer so obviously felt about Nick. She felt Trent's arm tighten around her waist and turned to him. His spicy eyes twinkled and he gave her a quick wink before spinning her back into his arms to start dancing again.

For the briefest of moments, Linda looked at Trent and began to wonder if she already had.

After two slow dances, they danced another fast set. Linda fanned her face with her hand. "All this dancing is getting to me."

Trent took off his tie and stuffed it into his hip

pocket then rolled up his sleeves to his elbows. "This is harder than doing the obstacle course we have to run to qualify yearly," he said. "Why don't we go outside for a minute and cool off?"

"Let's," Linda agreed. "I don't think anyone will miss us."

"Let me just grab my jacket," Trent said. He retrieved it from the chair before they headed to the front door. Outside it was already dark, the moon just rising. "I didn't think it was this late," he said looking at the starry sky.

Linda crossed her arms in front of her and looked up. For a moment they stood silent on the top porch step just looking at the night sky. Trent slung his jacket over his left shoulder, suspending it from two fingers. He watched as Linda closed her eyes and breathed in the crisp spring air and wondered if she knew just how beautiful she looked in the silver light.

"Let's walk," he said touching the curve of her elbow. She let her hands fall to her side. He slid his hand down her arm to her hand and entwined his fingers with hers. He held her hand loosely and it would have only taken a simple movement for Linda to withdraw her hand from his, but she didn't.

They walked down the steps and across the lawn that sprawled toward a small stream with a patch of farmland behind it. A line of evergreens created separation between the restaurant grounds and the fields making it seem like a black carrier against the lighter shade of the night sky. Ahead a white gazebo offered them a place to sit down and they headed right for it.

Again Linda felt a sense of comfort and turned to meet Trent's eyes as they took a step up into the structure in unison. *What is it about a man with a jacket slung over his shoulder that makes him look so sexy?* she wondered. At about the same time he took the jacket in both hands and placed it around her shoulders, leaving one arm there. The spicy scent of his cologne rising from the jacket now enveloped her, giving rise to the sense that they were on the brink of starting something that might not be wise. They weren't dancing; his arm had no reason to be around her, but, to her, it felt right.

The gazebo was made entirely of wood and their steps echoed as they walked slowly to the bench that ran around all five sides. She started to sit down but he stopped her by turning and putting both arms around her.

"It's probably dirty and you may ruin your dress," he said, taking the jacket from her shoulders and placing it down on the bench. "Now it's safe."

Linda nodded, feeling like he had just thrown his cape down over a puddle of water in the street so she could walk over it. Maybe chivalry wasn't entirely dead after all. Once she was settled onto the bench, he sat down beside her. His forearms rested casually on his thighs, his hands clasped between his spread knees in a typical male pose.

"I have to ask you," Linda said, "what did you mean when you said it was your sister and you against the rings? And did I hear right? You called her Pooch. Is that a family nickname or something?"

Trent snorted his laugh and, looking down at his hands, shook his head. "It's kind of a long story."

"Now I'm intrigued."

He leaned back and rested his elbows back onto the railing that ran along the wall. "You'll be sorry you asked."

"Now I'm really intrigued."

"Okay then. I called her Mooch, not Pooch. It's short for Allamuchy."

"Family name?"

"State park."

Linda furrowed her brow, clearly confused.

"Mom and Dad were flower children from the seventies. The peace-and-love thing was very important to them throughout their marriage even after it wasn't trendy to be flower children any more. Everything they did had a very deep meaning to them." He rolled his eyes. "And I mean everything."

"So they named your sister after a state park?"

"They named all of us after something."

"Somer and Trent seem normal enough, but Allamuchy?"

Trent straightened and turned slightly toward her. "Here's where it gets a little strange. Mom wanted to be able to commemorate the exact places in which she and dad planned every addition to their family, so to do that, she named us after the place they were when they decided to have each child."

Linda's brows furrowed deeper. "I think I understand."

"Somerville, Trenton, and Allamuchy," he pronounced. "None of us will ever forget where we were planned as additions to the Archer family."

Linda fell silent for a moment as if processing the information. Then her mouth opened in a perfectly mimed "Oh" when she totally understood. "Very . . . quaint."

"That's one way of putting it. We don't use our full names much, although I think I got the best of the deal."

"You did."

"And Mooch got the worst. Partly due to my renaming her early in life."

"That's mean."

"It's a brother thing. I had to do it. It's in the Brother Code of Ethics."

She laughed. "I guess that's one book I didn't read."

"Not allowed. Boys only."

Linda reacted almost involuntarily and stiffened. "Oh." She stood, picked up his jacket from the bench, and handed it to him. "I guess that mind-set starts a lot earlier than I realized."

He stood and took it from her. "I didn't mean anything by it. I was only making a joke."

She blew out a long breath of air. "I know," she conceded. "Not your fault. It was just a knee-jerk reaction. It seems lately I've been knocking on the door of the Boys Only Club and getting told I still have to stay outside."

"What happened?"

She waved off his question. "It's not important."

"It is if it affects you like that. Can I help somehow?"

"I have to sort it out. I know that women and men have equal opportunity to everything, but . . ." she stopped, unsure of how to say it.

"But what?"

He reached over and touched her hand. The contact made her heartbeat rise. "But I still feel the competition. I'm good at what I do, real good, and I know I should be grateful." Her gaze wandered over his shoulder as she tried to congeal all that she was feeling into coherent words.

"But the guys at work sometimes think you've gotten where you are because you're a woman instead of in spite of it," Trent filled in.

"I know it sounds absolutely ridiculous. This is the twenty-first century and all that macho jealousy should be a thing of the past." Her lips trembled in anger. "But sometimes I still feel it and I feel like I have to prove to them that I'm quite capable of being their equal. And I feel that I need more focus, more dedication, and no distractions to do it." Trent's brown eyes confronted hers with a combination of understanding and uncertainty. "Darn," she said, feeling utterly foolish to have admitted such a thing. "I feel like an idiot for saying that now." She dropped her chin and looked at the back of her hands. "I probably need therapy."

"I imagine there are still a fair number of jerks out there who still think only men can rule, so to speak, so never apologize for the way you feel."

She lifted her face and found herself only a few inches from Trent's. "Thanks. I won't." She smiled feeling genuinely better.

"Glad to help. Besides, I think strong, confident women are sexy."

She looked at his lips as he spoke. *Don't let him kiss you. If you do, you're in for one big problem,* her heart warned. "I guess that means you aren't threatened by them."

"Not in the least." He began moving his fingers softly on her bare shoulders. "You said you were angry that I didn't ask if I could kiss you earlier." His gaze roamed her face before settling on her eyes. "So I'll ask you this time. Can I kiss you?"

"We probably shouldn't have come out here," she said, biting her lip and turning her head away from his gaze.

In response he raised his hand, his fingers caressing her cheek so softly that a shaft of liquid fire seemed to burn her skin wherever he touched.

"Probably not," he agreed, his voice husky.

"We should go back in, then."

"Just lead the way."

She remained right where she was, her gaze still on his mouth. "You first."

He shook his head. "Not until you answer the question. Can I kiss you?"

"Why do you want to?"

"Because something happened when I met you in the church yesterday. When I sat down beside you in that pew—"

Suddenly she leaned forward and kissed him, cutting off the rest of his words. The kiss was gentle, unhurried, and tentative. When she pulled back, her expression seemed to apologize.

His smile came slowly, sensually. "When I sat down beside you in that pew," he continued, his voice low, "I suddenly wanted to know what it would be like to kiss you."

"I think I said yes," she said with a smile.

He smiled back as he slanted his head, his left arm slipping around her waist, his right hand moving to caress the back of her head until she tipped her head sideways to accommodate him. His lips took hers with gentle circular nudges as the provocative seconds passed. He forced his kiss to remain gentle, swallowing the sounds of pleasure that wanted to escape from his throat.

For him, she kissed the way she looked: confident, thorough, and experienced. She had some practice at this, he thought, and it would be fun to find out how much. Just as he was about to pull away, she flung her arms around his neck and kissed him hard.

Surprised, he lifted his head for a moment. Her eyes were heavy leaded circles of shadow, but her breath was warm on his face. "And now that I know how you kiss, I don't think you have to ask me first anymore," she said.

His warm palms now contoured her ribs. "Good, because asking sure does waste time getting down to the good stuff."

His comment brought common sense rushing back to Linda. What in the world had she just done? She stepped back and out of his arms, watching the expression on his face change from pleasure to confusion.

"I'm sorry. This should not have happened. I think we just got caught up in the mood of a wedding. It's very romantic to watch a bride and groom together. So different from the ways things are in our world of law and order."

"What happened wasn't in any textbook I read at the academy," he countered.

"It doesn't have to be. We are both intelligent enough to know that before this goes any farther, we need to understand that this is more atmosphere and occasion than anything else."

Trent tilted his head, appearing to think about what she said before drawing in a deep breath and jamming his hands into his pants pockets. "So I guess that means we need to get back inside."

"I suppose it does."

As they walked back to the reception, silence hung between them. Trent checked his watch. It was 8 o'clock. He only had a few hours left to come up with something to keep Linda with him until he could figure out what he was going to do about her.

Chapter Six

Back at the reception inside Trent tried to avoid his sister, but Ali had been looking for him for over an hour. She crossed her arms over her chest. "Sphinx pink is not your color."

Trent's brow furrowed. "Huh?"

Ali reached out and rubbed her thumb across Trent's lips. She angled it to him. "Trendy, but too light for you." Her lips pursed in a sign of pique.

Trent scrubbed the back of his hand across his mouth. "You're right." He looked over at Linda. She had her fingertips to her lips to hide any smears. "I'm more the fire-engine-red type."

Ali grabbed his upper arm. "You'll excuse us for a minute, won't you, Linda?" She pulled him to the side of the dance floor before Linda could answer. "Where have you two been?" She flicked out her forefinger and hit the end of his nose, something their mother did to get their attention when they were children.

"Ow, that still hurts as much as it ever did," Trent said, rubbing the tip of his nose.

"No kidding. Answer the question."

"We went out for air."

Ali put her hand on her hip and clenched her jaw. "Is that what they call it now?"

Trent looked over her shoulder. Linda was dancing with some guy in a tan suit. She saw him and smiled.

"I kissed her. So what?" he asked.

"So what?" Ali threw up her hands. "So what? Have you forgotten about 'the Curse'?" She emphasized the word with a pair of air quotes.

Trent dismissed her with a snort. "You have got to be kidding. I am not in to fairy tales today."

He started to walk away when Ali's voice stopped him. "I swear if you end up married I'll never forgive you."

"Relax, Mooch," Trent said after spinning back to face her. "It's a ring. A little blue stone set in gold. It's not a love amulet."

Ali hitched her thumb toward Somer and Nick. "Tell them that."

Trent tapped Mr. Tan Suit on the shoulder. "I'll take it from here." He grabbed Linda's hand and spun her away from her dance partner. A slow dance came on and he reverted to a waltz position with six inches of space between them.

Linda glanced at Ali, who was glaring. "Something happen with your sister?"

He looked at Ali and gave her an exaggerated smile. "Family thing," he said, returning his gaze to Linda.

"You don't have to tell me unless you want to, but from the look on both your faces, I really want to know."

He saw playfulness come into her eyes and smiled. "Why not? Technically you're part of it anyway."

Linda's eyes grew wide. "I am? What do I have to do with your family?"

He took a step back, extended his arm, and turned her in a quick circle before pulling her back into his arms. "That was for Ali's benefit," he whispered into her ear.

Linda's eyes made a quick tour of his face, lingering a bit on his lips before returning to his eyes. "What is going on? If you're going to use me to get even with your sister for something, I don't think I want any part of it."

"Don't go all cop on me. I have every intention of asking if you want in first." He nestled her against his frame. "It's not my sister that's the problem. I didn't finish telling you about it when we were outside, but it's my grandmother Vicky's ring that's causing all the commotion."

"Now I'm really confused," Linda confessed. She grimaced. "It must be some kind of diamond."

"It's a sapphire, actually."

"Oh, like in something borrowed, something blue."

"Not quite that easy." He danced her off to the edge of the dance floor away from the blaring speakers the DJ used so they could talk more easily. "A year or so ago mom had this idea that she wanted grandchildren. So she gave each of us one of Grandma Vicky's rings and told us to go out and find our true loves."

"Just like that? Go out and find your true love?" Linda flicked her hand in the air.

Trent mimicked her gesture. "Just like that."

"Did the ring come with an instruction manual on how you were supposed to do that?"

Trent shook his head. "Not a word."

Linda snickered. "Good luck hunting, then."

"Are you scoffing at my family's legend?" Trent teased.

"Ah—yeah!"

Again Trent spun her out and pulled her back, settling his hands on her waist. "How do you explain then that Nick came into Somer's life right afterward?"

"Coincidence?"

"He settled her back against his hip. "Karma," he corrected. "Their relationship is too pure, too perfect to be random." He nodded and then settled his chin against her cheek. "Yep, it was karma."

Linda glanced over his shoulder at Somer and Nick

talking to Tess Archer. "Your mother doesn't really think that your grandmother's ring actually brought Nick and Somer together, does she?"

Trent neatly exchanged sides with her in two steps. "She sure does."

"And your sister thinks that's why we went outside and that's why . . ." She stopped.

"I kissed you?" There was a sexy glint in Trent's eyes.

"Did you tell her it was just the excitement, the aura of a wedding and the like?"

"Is that all it was?"

Linda backed up and put distance between their bodies. "Do you think otherwise?"

Trent's gaze roamed to her mouth and stayed there. "I thought it was nice. Very nice."

He saw a smile touch Linda's lips then light her eyes, and at that moment, he thought he'd never seen a woman more beautiful. Her hair was slightly messy from being outside. She hadn't had time to fix it. And her lipstick was all gone from his kisses. When he first saw her yesterday, he had thought she needed to put on some lipstick, but he had been wrong. She didn't need to be perfect like a model in one of those bride's magazines. She had a natural beauty that surpassed that stuff.

The music stopped and he took his hands from her waist. They stood there looking at each other in silence for a while.

"Looks like that was the last dance," Linda said as she saw Somer and Nick begin to go from table to table to say good-bye to their wedding guests. "All that's left is for Somer to toss her bouquet before they leave for their honeymoon."

"How are you getting home?" Trent asked her.

"I think the limo service is going to drop the wedding attendants at their homes or hotels."

"I can do it," he volunteered.

"Don't trouble yourself."

"No trouble. My car's here. I dropped it off earlier so I wouldn't have to rely on anyone to take me home."

Linda bit down on her lower lip as if trying to decide. She smiled impishly. "Okay, but first let's make sure your sister sees us leave together."

"You're not going to try to catch the bouquet?"

She waved her hands in the air. "No way. I'm not going to tempt fate and have your grandmother's ring get me. Besides, it'll be more fun if we go early and leave your sister trying to figure out why."

Trent's eyes narrowed. "You're on!" He grabbed her hand and towed her toward the head table to collect her things. There they made a theatrical production out of leaving together, making sure Ali saw everything.

"Look at Mooch," Trent whispered, hooking his arm around Linda's waist. "She can barely keep her eyes on Somer."

Linda looked over in time to see Somer turn her back to the group of single ladies standing in the middle of the dance floor and toss her bouquet over her head in their direction. She smothered a grin as she saw the flowers glance off Ali's fingertips and land in the hands of an older woman who whooped in triumph as she caught it.

Ali clamped her hands to her hips and mouthed "See what you made me do?" as the woman grabbed the hand of the hunky guy who had caught the garter thrown by Nick and then headed for a chair in the middle of the dance floor for the obligatory photo.

"Looks like your sister isn't too happy about the outcome of the bouquet-garter toss thing," Linda commented.

"She'll get over it," Trent said. "That's Aunt Barbara who caught the bouquet, and that's Mike Corbel who caught the garter. Aunt Barb will make a production out of the photo op and Ali can console Mike later. Everyone wins!"

"Guess so," Linda said as Aunt Barbara sat down on the chair and hiked her skirt up over her knees, waiting for poor Mike to slip the garter on her leg as per tradition.

When they got outside they heard the DJ say, "And every inch past her knee means ten years of wedded bliss for Somer and Nick."

Linda stopped right before getting into Nick's car. "Now if the custom rings true, how many years do you suppose Nick and Somer will have of wedded bliss?"

Trent snorted. "You don't know Aunt Barb. Is she has her way, about a hundred."

They pulled up in front of the Hilton Garden Inn. "Home sweet home," Trent quipped, turning off the car.

"For tonight," Linda said.

In the silence that followed, they looked up at the stars through the moonroof of the car. In the stillness, the only sound seemed to be the soft rustle of leaves in the wind. After a few minutes, Linda turned and reached for the door handle.

Trent grabbed her other hand. "Wait." In the starlight, he saw the surprise on her face.

"Do you need something, Trent?" she asked.

He pressed his lips together and nodded. "Actually, yes. You can slap me later if you'd like, but you did tell me I didn't have to ask anymore."

He pulled her to him by her hand, surprised but pleased when she allowed it. He took her chin with his fingertips, urging her not to move as he moved toward her. He hesitated for a moment, his eyes searching her face for refusal. When he found none, he buried her lips beneath his in a kiss that was totally different from the one they shared on the grounds at the reception. This one was significant, potent, like a train coming at her at full force.

She answered with a force of her own, telling herself she would only answer his kiss just enough to make it memorable and then let go. But she had scarcely put her arms around him as much as her position in the car would allow when she knew beyond all sense of reason that she was going to be the one to remember this kiss for a very long time.

Perhaps it was the tight quarters that made the heat rise around them or maybe it was the excitement of the chase that made her want to explore something this totally physical. Certainly it was the whole wedding experience that probably put them in this frame of mind; the countless times their gazes had locked over the course of the evening, words that evoked romance, the looks of attraction and curiosity.

Trent broke away slowly, ending the passionate kiss with a return of his lips to hers for a sweet, quick touch before smiling.

"I knew it," he said, shaking his head, his ragged breath rumbling soft next to her ear. "It wasn't just a fluke."

"What wasn't?" Her own voice sounded throaty to her.

"The way I feel about you when I kiss you." He took her hand in his and pressed it to his chest. "Feel that?" His chest rose and fell while inside his heart beat a furious rhythm as though it wanted to break through his skin. "It's been doing that all day whenever I looked at you and allowed myself to think about kissing you. Then in the garden it picked up speed and hasn't stopped since."

"It's the wedding thing. It makes you feel all hearts and flowers," she said, inching toward the door.

"I don't think that's it."

She turned back to him, considering the countless complications another kiss could bring for both of them. She looked up at the stars, in his eyes, at his mouth, and considered her choices. There was really only one.

"You're a great guy," she said.

"How do you know? We're virtual strangers still."

She smiled. "A good cop always goes with her instincts."

"Or his."

"Or his," she agreed. "And some of my instincts tell me it's time to go." She leaned forward to give him a quick kiss on the cheek.

"Don't."

He pulled back. Not jerking away, not even forcefully. He simply retreated and she understood that neither was able to hone in on the mixed signals being sent and received.

"I'm sorry," she said.

"Don't be. Want me to walk you in?"

She shook her head.

"You will be at the brunch tomorrow, right?"

She nodded. "Sure. Wouldn't miss it." He began to get out but she opened the car door herself. He didn't look at her when she got out. She stood outside at the curb with her hand on the door handle and waited until he opened the automatic window from his side. "Thanks for being a terrific partner, Trent Archer."

"Right back at you, Linda Wolff," he acknowledged.

He refrained from looking at her in the rearview mirror for too long as he drove away. When he finally did glance at it, she had already gone inside.

He blew out a long breath of air. She was the kind of woman he'd been looking for for a long time. At least he thought so. She had a way about her, a spirit strong yet gentle, demanding yet reciprocal. She seemed to be the type that deserved someone who would appreciate her for the person she was as well as encourage her to follow her dreams to the person she wanted to be. As a fellow officer, she undoubtedly understood what it meant to be on the force and would respect his commitment to it. And it was all wrapped up in a package that looked darn good.

He definitely wanted to get to know her better to explore the possibilities. He'd start by sticking close to her at the brunch reception tomorrow.

Chapter Seven

The first voice Linda heard when she swung the doors open at Manhattan South on Monday afternoon when her shift was over was that of the desk sergeant.

"Hey, Wolff, you got a visitor."

Glancing around the station, she didn't see anyone she knew. She took off her cap and tucked it under her arm. "Who?" she asked, checking the desk for messages. She waved her temporary partner to go on without her.

"Some guy. He's been here since about ten this morning."

She looked up the right hall and down the left. She raised her hands and shook her head. "Must be gone."

"He asked where he could get a cup of coffee so I sent him to the break room."

Linda prickled. "You sent a civ to the back?" she asked the desk sergeant, her tone terse. "With every-thing that happens here in the city, you just let some stranger stroll in here and wander into the break room? You know you broke every protocol ever issued, don't you?"

The desk sergeant looked up from the report he had been reading. "Relax, Wolff, he said he was your boyfriend. I figured you patted him down and did a background check, so he was safe enough."

A patrolman and detective at the board behind the desk turned more fully toward her and snickered. "Wolff, you didn't tell us you got a boyfriend," the detective said.

"I don't," she countered. "But if I did, you'd both be the last ones to know."

"You're going to break the hearts of everyone in Homicide if word like that gets around. Talk is that you've put in your transfer papers for the opening at the 71st in Brooklyn."

"Talk is cheap," she said, raising her hand in a salute. Uncomfortable beneath their needling scrutiny, she took the one message that was for her and headed for the break room. She read it as she walked. It was from Trent wondering if she forgot about the brunch with a request for her to call. It was dated yesterday afternoon.

She smiled at his persistence. She didn't leave him her number, but he had managed to track down at the precinct in which she worked. Nice detective work, but totally wasted on her. They had been paired for a wedding. A one-day fix-up and nothing more. She didn't have time to invest in a relationship of any kind. She wasn't going to be a beat cop all her career. She had a plan. It would take hard work with no distractions of any kind to get to where she wanted to be.

And today's plan started with checking out this visitor and sending him or her on their way so she could audit the 7:30 class at NYU this evening. Dr. Kenneth Rory was scheduled as a guest lecturer on the Technique of Polygraph Examination. His vast experience in interrogation methods and the fact that he was considered the consummate expert witness in the field made this class one she did not want to miss.

She angled her watch to her eyes. She had about two hours to get rid of whomever it was who thought he or she knew her well enough to come to her job. Then she still had to shower, change, and get to the class.

She'd have to get rid of her visitor in less than five minutes if she was going to get to the university in time to find a seat in Dr. Rory's class.

She stopped at the door to the break room and looked inside. A few people stood around the thirty-cup coffeemaker set on the table across the room. A few others were at a desk leaning over a bunch of new NCIC alerts, coffee in hand.

But her visitor sat at the table right in front of the door. She blinked, surprised by his presence on her turf.

"Hello, Trent."

"Hello, Linda."

She headed for the coffeepot. Trent rose and followed her. He reached around and poured a cup for her before taking one for himself. Trying to look unaffected by his presence, she took hers and ambled over to a table. He sat down across from her.

"What are you doing here?" she asked.

Trent looked around the room. Everyone seemed to be looking at them. "Do I need a secret handshake or something to get in here?"

Linda sat stiffly at the table trying to keep her expression neutral. Trent wore a light blue shirt that contrasted rather nicely with his deep tan. His eyes danced with amusement and undisguised interest when he spoke.

"What are you doing here?" she asked again, trying to gather her warring emotions.

"Did you really expect me to just let you disappear after the weekend? After what we shared?"

"Don't try out your lines on me. They won't work." Or would they? The intense look in his eyes was tugging at her feminine side despite the fact that she was still in uniform.

"No lines. Really. I came here for a reason."

Linda leaned back in her chair. "It better be a good one because I still can't imagine why the desk sergeant let you back here."

"You missed the party yesterday, so you owe me brunch."

Linda didn't know whether to be relieved or disappointed. "It wasn't my party, so it didn't matter if I showed up or not," she explained.

"It mattered to me," he replied, holding her gaze.

Linda tried to give him a nonplussed look, but knew she failed by the way the muscles in the corners of her mouth fought to rise.

"Really?" she asked him, unsure why she had.

"Yes, really."

Now what was she supposed to say. She got up and went back to the coffeemaker. At the table she grabbed a few packets of sugar and dumped them in her coffee. As she stirred it, she wondered how she was going to choke it down. She never put sugar in her coffee. Trent seemed to make her do the strangest things when she was around him.

She brushed by him when she walked back to the table. He was wearing that same wonderful spicy aftershave that made her want to nuzzle his neck the way she had at the reception.

He looked around room again. Off and on a few people randomly checked on them. "I feel the tension in the air here. Is there someplace we can talk without it feeling like everyone is waiting to see what I say?"

She felt heat rush to her cheeks. "Are you going to say something you shouldn't?"

He opened his hands. "You never know. I came here today to find out if I scared you and that's why you blew off the brunch yesterday. If I did, I apologize. If I didn't, I kind of wonder what happened."

She shrugged. "I just didn't want you to think I was encouraging anything. I don't date cops much anymore."

"I sort of got that feeling. But it was brunch for wedding after-party, not a date. I thought we had a lot in common and I was looking forward to talking cop shop with you. That's all."

Stung by her total misreading of the situation, Linda looked down at her sickly sweet drink and took a healthy swig. She had to force herself not to spit it out. "Oh." It was all she could think of to say.

"And I'd still like to do that," Trent continued.

"Maybe some other time. I'm auditing a class tonight." She looked down at her watch and then rose. "And If I get out of this uniform right now, I still have time to stop at the bookstore and buy the textbook. You'll have to excuse me, Trent. It seems you came all the way to New York for nothing."

Trent stood and crossed his arms over his chest. "Heck of a note, isn't it?"

"What is?"

"I come all this way, wait all this time, and you're

making up an excuse to get rid of me. Didn't I impress you one bit with my tenacity?"

"I'm not making up an excuse. I really do have to get to class. Besides, you only want to talk shop. You said it yourself." She flung her arm out to the side. "There are about ten guys here who would love to tell you about themselves. Pick one."

Trent let his shoulders drop. "Okay, you got me. I didn't come here to talk shop. I can't help it. I like the heck out of you. I was disappointed you weren't at brunch and I came here to talk you into dinner." He took a couple of steps toward her and she retreated. Lowering his voice, he continued, "Something happened to me when I met you. I can't get you out of my mind."

"Give it up, Trent," Linda said. "This is not a pursuit and I am not the suspect. I'm flattered, really, but you're wasting your time."

"I'm not going to give up," he informed her quietly. "And I'm not much of a hunter and I don't consider you the prey."

Linda shook her head. "Forget it. I'm not falling for it."

"Not at first, anyway. But you will," Trent promised.

Linda couldn't help herself and let a smile break. Trent was impossible. "You are tenacious, I have to give you that." The tension between them suddenly dissolved as her smile grew wider.

Grinning, Trent slapped his hands together. "See? It's starting already."

"No, it's not," Linda said, trying more to convince herself than to convince him. She looked at her watch again. "And I'm late."

"Okay, I'll leave." He threw her a lock salute. "I'll see you around."

"Hillsborough is that way," Linda said, pointing to her left. "I don't think it's close enough for you to be seeing me around all that much."

Trent just shrugged and left.

Linda stared after him. His walk was cocky, brazen with squared shoulders and a confident stride. A few of the female officers in the room stopped talking and watched him leave, and she felt a tinge of jealousy when they did.

She rinsed what was left of the sugary sweet coffee from the mug and headed for the locker room. A three-hour lecture on the science of lie detectors should erase all remaining remnants of Trent Archer from her mind.

At least for the beginning of the evening, that was.

In the locker room, she tucked her hat on the top shelf of her locker. Then she unloaded her service revolver and stashed the clip before slipping the gun back into her holster on her belt. Then she unbuckled her belt and put it on the top locker shelf with her hat.

The band around her ponytail had been bothering

her all day so she ripped it out and ran her fingers through her hair, feeling the tension in her shoulders release. Her hair fell around her shoulders in a thick wave, lines from the rubber band sculpting curves into it. She looked into the mirror hung on her locker door. Presentable enough for a lecture, she decided.

"That guy is pretty cute."

The comment came from behind her. She turned in time to see an officer from her shift changing into her civvies.

She must have had a puzzled look on her face because the officer continued, "The guy in the break room. The cop from New Jersey."

Linda slipped a pale pink oversized shirt over her shoulders. "I guess," she said buttoning it, not wanting to make eye contact for fear more than neutrality showed in her eyes.

"Augie says he's your boyfriend."

Linda kicked off her work shoes and hung her uniform pants on one of the hooks and put on a pair of khakis. "Augie should spend more time finding out who is and who is not supposed to be wandering all over the station, and less time worrying about my personal life."

"So he is your boyfriend, then."

"No." Linda sat on the wooden bench between the rows of lockers. She took out a pair of brown sandals and eased her feet into them. "We were paired up for a wedding this weekend. That's all."

"So why'd he come to the precinct looking for you?"

"He didn't say," Linda lied. She checked her off-duty gun, slipped it into a small holster, and hooked it on the waistband of her slacks at the small of her back before standing and closing her locker. She gave the padlock a few turns to lock it and began to leave.

"You must have made an impression on him for him to come all the way to the city," her fellow officer said, not giving her a chance to close the subject. "Augie said he's been here for hours."

"So I'm told."

The gals in Narc think he's really cute."

"He's okay if you like the type."

"The man looks like Matthew McConaughey."

Linda tried to keep her voice even. "Maybe in the dark." She began to leave.

"Peterson says if you don't want him, she'll take him."

Linda turned back to her. "Doesn't anyone have anything better to talk about?"

"Not today," the officer said, slamming her locker shut.

Chapter Eight

Trent saw Linda as soon as she walked into the bookstore. He watched her for a few minutes, just absorbing the way she looked. Her extra-long pink shirt curved nicely over her backside and thighs. Loose enough to be comfortable, it also served to hide her off-duty weapon, which he'd bet a week's pay was tucked at her back just like it was at the wedding. Her dark hair curled around her shoulders glinting as the artificial light painted it with streaks of what looked like amber fire that mesmerized him.

Luckily he'd guessed right about her using the closest bookstore to get the textbook she needed. Happily he intended to take full advantage of his powers of deduction.

"Fancy meeting you here," he said, savoring her

reaction as she entered the fiction section. Linda's shock showed on her face when she recognized his voice. "What are the odds of us shopping at the very same bookstore?" he asked.

Linda's eyes widened. Trent stood only a foot away from her, brazenly male and completely confident. The girls in Narc were right. He did look like Matthew McConaughey. In any light. The book she was holding fell from her hands.

Both bent down to pick it up at the same time. Their heads banged together.

"Ouch." Linda rocked back on her heels.

"Right about that," Trent said, rubbing his brow. "I guess it's true about great minds thinking alike."

"You have a hard head," Linda said, running her fingertips across her forehead.

"I thought you did."

"You followed me here?" Linda accused, grabbing the book from the floor between them.

"No, I got here first. I wanted to get the newest James Patterson to read on the train home."

"Do you know the odds of us meeting at this particular bookstore? There is one on just about every corner in this part of the city. Honestly, come on."

"I guess they are rather phenomenal, then," Trent admitted, enjoying watching her. "But I do believe in fate."

"Like you believe in that ring thing you told me about at the wedding?" she countered. "I don't think so." She glared, apparently hoping to make him uncomfortable. He didn't bite. She turned and walked toward the reference books with Trent right behind her. "Stop following me. The fiction section is back where you were."

"Did I tell you how much I like feisty women?" Trent said in hot pursuit as she ducked down a narrow aisle across from the foreign language section.

Thinking she'd lost him by twisting and turning up and down several aisles, she finally made it to the reference books. Looking over her shoulder, she saw no one coming her way. Stooping, she located the book she needed on a lower shelf just as she heard someone behind her clear his throat. Scowling, Linda swiveled on her heels and saw a pair of brown shoes next to her. Her gaze lifted up the leg of faded denim jeans to sleeves of a white shirt and upward to a satisfied smile that seemed to take up a whole face.

"I thought I could use a dictionary too," Trent said. "For better spelling on reports."

Linda rose. "Stop it."

"It's a crime now to try to improve oneself?" He held up his fingers in a sign of peace.

"You did follow me here, didn't you?"

"No, I didn't. I used my detective skills to figure out where you might go when you tried to blow me off at the station." He smiled again when she narrowed her blue eyes. She sure looked beautiful when she was angry.

She put the book she needed on the shelf and crossed her arms over her chest. "Okay, it seems I am not going to get anywhere near class tonight. What exactly is it that you want Trent?"

"Dinner. I've been in the city since around eleven this morning and I haven't eaten anything substantial."

"There are snacks in the vending machines at the station."

"They are probably a hundred years old too. You'd let a fellow officer starve just to prove a point?"

"I may."

"Wouldn't that amount to manslaughter?"

His eyes showed her the mischief inside. He wasn't about to let her off easy. He was so tall and easygoing that she couldn't take her eyes off him. The indefinable aura about him seemed to linger from the wedding. Whatever it was that attracted her to him was still there, and she still was not immune to it.

"All right, you win." She held out her hand. "Dinner and then home. Deal?"

He took it gladly. "For today."

She walked with him to the checkout, pleased that he shortened his long, lanky stride for her benefit. There he reached for his wallet.

"Please, no," she said. "The book's a bit pricey, and besides, you're buying dinner." She put her hand on his to stop him from pulling out any money.

The contact generated immediate heat where her fingers touched his arm. It surprised her almost as much as the heat rising on her cheeks because of it. She looked up and then quickly looked away from his smiling eyes.

"Dinner it is," he said as the cashier finished the transaction and they walked outside. "Where to?" he asked once they hit the sidewalk.

"We're not dressed for anything fancy, so I think I know the perfect place. Like Italian?"

"Doesn't everyone?"

She took Trent to Ristamore on Mulberry Street in the heart of Little Italy. A no-nonsense spot with brick walls, a tin ceiling, bare tables, and oversized Italian posters on the walls, it was a casual place where they could relax and blend in.

She didn't want anyone from the station to see her. A few weeks ago one of the detectives starting seeing a girl from Connecticut and was teased unmercifully for "shopping out of town." She didn't need or want the ribbing.

She wondered briefly if the camaraderie at Trent's station was the same, but dismissed the thought almost as quickly as it had come. There was no sense thinking about something that wasn't going to work out anyway.

A quick look around told her she was right. She didn't recognize anyone and relaxed a little.

They followed the hostess to a table in the back. Trent held out the chair and invited Linda to sit down first. He sat opposite her.

"Nice place," he said, opening the oversized menu he'd accepted from the waiter. "Anyone who can't find something they like on this menu isn't paying enough attention."

They listened to the day's specials before asking for more time to decide.

Trent juggled the voluminous menu. "With all these choices—marsalas, parmigianas, oregentatas, sorentinas—it's hard to decide. What's good here?"

"Everything," Linda assured.

"Okay, then." He closed his eyes and circled his forefinger above the menu before stabbing at the center of the left side. "Pollo ala Paseano," he read. "Boneless chicken in a garlic rosemary sauce with sausage and roasted peppers." He looked up. "What about you?"

"I don't think I'll throw caution to the wind and let my fingers do the walking. I haven't had the Sicilian-style Chilean sea bass before, so I think I'll try that," Linda replied.

They passed on cocktails and ordered just water with lemon along with their meals. The waiter brought them a basket with an assortment of fresh-baked breads along with a small dish of seasoned oil in which to dip them. He watched Linda take a sip of the tart, lemony water the waiter set down in front of her and allowed the quiet to filter between them.

Only when he saw her shoulders drop and de-cided the tension was finally releasing did he ease the conversation to something a little more personal than what was on the menu.

"How much trouble did I cause you by coming to the city and hanging out at the station to wait for you?"

Linda scowled. "A ton. I wasn't in the locker room five minutes when the interrogation started."

"So did I pass muster?"

Rolling her eyes Linda said, "I suppose so. A few of the girls in Narc think so at least."

Trent grinned, squaring his shoulders with the compliment. "You don't say."

"Not so fast. You have to remember they work a lot and don't get out all that much socially."

"Touché," Trent conceded, picking up his glass in a mock salute.

"It looked like your head was swelling. Couldn't have that," Linda explained.

Trent shook his head. "Always on duty."

"What do you mean?"

"Control the situation. Isn't that what we're taught at the academy?"

Linda looked down at her half-eaten piece of bread. She appeared to mull over his question. She looked back at him and held his gaze. "You're right. I was."

"I didn't say it to be right. I said it because I want you to relax. You're out of uniform and off duty, Officer Wolff. So let's just be Trent and Linda for the rest of the evening."

"We could try."

Trent suddenly frowned. "Maybe this is none of my business, but was it the attack on Nick that keeps you on edge all the time?"

Linda visibly cringed. "I don't talk about it much to anyone."

"Why?"

"I messed up."

"And you don't like to admit it."

Linda shook her head. "No, I don't like to be reminded of it."

"But you need an outlet. We all do. Friends talk." He gestured. "Here I am." She didn't say anything more. "Well?" he prompted.

"Who do you talk to about things?" she asked.

"I'll let you change the subject, but just note that we're going to be getting back to you in a second." Trent studied Linda for a moment. The tension in her face had disappeared. "I talk to family about some things; my friend Zak about others."

"Man things," Linda cut in.

Trent nodded. "I don't think Mom or my sisters want to hear about sports."

"Or about your latest conquests."

Trent grimaced. "Or them."

Linda laughed. "Just how many of them have there been?"

"A few," Trent hedged. "Present company not included in the count, of course."

"Better not," she warned, laughing again.

"I wouldn't think of it," Trent replied, enjoying her amusement and wishing he could count her among those he had had a serious relationship. She was pretty, very pretty—too pretty to hide inside a structured dark blue uniform and underneath a regulation stiff cap. The candlelight played with her dark hair, bringing out the red and gold highlights she probably didn't even realize she had. And there was warmth inside her eyes, making the blue seem the color of warm Caribbean waters, warmth he could wrap himself around forever. "Your colleagues respect you too."

"How do you know that?"

"I saw it in their eyes." He picked up his glass and lifted it in acknowledgment.

"You wouldn't know it from the way they gave me the business about you."

"If they didn't joke around with you, it would mean they didn't care. It would mean you were just part of the furniture."

"Is that what you do in New Jersey?"

Trent nodded. "It's universal. We don't mess with someone we overlook. NYC cops are no different, I'm sure."

Their dinners came and Trent waited until the waiter left before speaking again. "Now let's ease this conversation back to you. Why a cop? Why not something more . . ."

"Ladylike?"

"That's not what I meant. More conventional?"

"Sounds the same to me," Linda said with the hint of a smile. Trent started to apologize, but she cut him off with a wave of her hand. "In a way, for me, it was the most conventional thing for me to do. Dad was a cop; mom joined the Army right out of high school and became a nurse, although she is semiretired now. My brother works for the FBI down in Quantico. I just fell into place."

"You said your dad was also a police officer. Is he retired now?"

Linda looked down at her plate. "He's not with us. He got caught in 9/11 at the Trade Center."

With a grimace Trent said, "I am sorry. Open mouth, insert foot. I should have known."

She looked up from her plate and into his eyes. "There was no way for you to have known."

"Then I shouldn't have been so insensitive as to not have considered the fact that every police officer or emergency responder may have been on duty that day. I could have phrased my questions better. Sometimes, despite everything, we seem to distance ourselves from the reality of that day. I guess it's because we don't truly want to believe in something that evil."

He mulled over the next question he wanted to ask her. Linda didn't seem angry or defensive about his question. If anything he felt she was trusting, and it made his heart soar a little. He didn't want to interfere with the good vibes that were starting between them, so he stepped on eggshells as he tried to find out a little more about her life.

"What was he like?" Trent asked.

Linda hesitated for a moment then said quietly, "Old-school. He never got a degree or anything, so he was mostly a beat cop. But a good one."

"I'm sure he was."

"Looking back, I don't think he ever wanted to do anything else, really. He loved the streets."

"Most old-school guys do," Trent agreed.

"Mom wanted him to retire in the worst way in 1998, but he wanted to stay five more years." Rubbing her brow she looked past him. "He refused. I remember them having terrible fights about it. Then 9/11 happened and it was too late for anything."

"Were you on the force then too?"

Linda nodded. "I had a year in, but still felt like I was fresh out of the academy. But I was off duty and on vacation that day. Safely tucked away in a hotel in Hawaii." She pressed her lips together and let out a long breath of air. "I should have been there."

"Don't think that way," Trent urged. "Lots of people were lucky that day. You were just one of them."

Linda shrugged. "I can't look at it like that. Dad died a hero and I was still asleep."

Trent shook his head. "Stop. It wasn't your fault. It was just the way the cards fell. It very well could have been the other way around."

She still felt guilty about being away that day. That

explained a lot about Linda and her dedication and commitment to the force. He wanted to help her somehow, but didn't know what to do.

"I flew back as soon as I could, but it took days for air traffic to get back to normal. By the time I got home, mom had it all under control. It was as if someone flicked on a light switch. She was amazing. That's why . . ." Linda hesitated, unsure whether to confide much more to Trent. But the understanding in his warm brown eyes made her go on. "That's why I stayed on even though Mom asked me to leave the force. I had to stay. I had a mission now."

"It took a lot of courage for you to do that."

Linda waited until the waiter refilled her water before speaking. "It felt more like the right thing to do than the brave thing to do." She toyed with her glass feeling some of the heaviness she had carried around with her since that day lift a bit. "Mom moved to Virginia to be closer to my brother a few years ago. She works part-time at Walter Reed to help care for the wounded soldiers who come back from Iraq and Afghanistan."

When she looked back at Trent, he could see the sadness in her eyes. He couldn't help himself. He reached out and took her hand. "She sounds amazing," he said. *Like her daughter*, he almost added.

His hand was warm on hers. She held his gaze and searched his somber features. It was no line, no attempt to get closer to her. He meant what he had said.

It would be wonderful to simply lean forward and kiss him, Linda thought. It was nice to talk to someone who understood. Maybe Trent could help her let go and trust again without worrying if everything would be taken away in the blink of an eye.

But he was a cop too. Two people with the same dangerous jobs should not be in a relationship. It would be double the worry and double the heartache if something went wrong.

Reality settled in around her. She wouldn't commit to a relationship with him. It was too dangerous for her. She knew about loss. She couldn't go through it again. Slowly she pulled her hand free.

"I should get going. Thanks for a lovely dinner."

Trent looked at his empty hand, still in the center of the table. He could feel her draw up the walls that had come down so briefly. *Be patient*, he told himself.

"And I do have to catch the train," he said. He got up, walked around the table, and pulled the chair gently back as she rose. "We'll get you a cab. Once you're tucked inside, I'll get one of my own."

"We can share one," she volunteered.

"Do you live near Penn Station?"

She shook her head. "Brooklyn"

He smiled. "Close enough."

Chapter Nine

The cab pulled up to the curb along a line of brownstones. Trent paid the cabbie and asked him to wait. He didn't get to the other side of the cab in time. Linda was already out and on the sidewalk.

"Which one?" he asked.

"There."

Linda pointed to the only Queen Anne–style brownstone set among the sharp lines of the Romanesque buildings that dominated the street. The delicate curves and soft arches of Linda's building contrasted with the rock-faced Roman brick surrounding it. Much like the woman who lived there, the softly feminine nature of Linda's brownstone communicated a feeling of quiet power.

"Nice," Trent said, walking up the steps with her. "Yours?"

"The family's. Mom didn't want to sell it when she moved to Virginia, so I'm like the caretaker until she's ready." She glanced at the cab idling at the curb. "I'd ask you in to see it, but the meter's running." She put her key in the lock and turned it open.

He reached around her and swept the door open. "I've put in some overtime last week. I'd love to see the house."

He bounded down the steps and back to the curb. There he pulled out a couple of twenties and handed them to the cab driver. "Just a deposit. Don't leave. I'll just be a minute." The cabbie nodded. Trent took the steps up to the brownstone's front door two at a time to where Linda was waiting for him.

Inside she snapped on the entry light. Even the artificial lighting couldn't hide the details. A hallway with rick dark wood and a stained-glass window greeted him. He knew all about the lonely hours a cop's wife or girlfriend endured. He guessed Linda's mother carefully brought the rich wood to life to pass the time.

"Quick tour," Linda said, tossing her bag onto the leather chair set just inside the door next to a coat rack. She pointed to the right. "The stairs lead up to the two floors above and down to the basement. This floor has the living room, dining room, kitchen, a study, and two baths. Second floor: two bedrooms, two baths. Third floor: one bedroom, a sort of sitting room, and one bath."

"Yours?"

"I staked it out when we moved here when I was ten. Over the years, I just stayed there. The basement has a lot of rooms framed out, but we never finished them. I guess they'll stay that way until someone buys the place in the future when Mom is ready to sell it."

Trent shrugged. "Too bad. This place is great."

A phone rang somewhere in the distance. "Take a quick look around if you'd like," Linda said as she went to answer it. There was a soft click as the door to the study shut.

Trent sighed and ran a hand through his hair. What in the world was he trying to do? He knew the answer to that question. Linda was the kind of woman he'd been searching for for a long time. At least he thought so. Just his luck that she was a tough cop who he sensed thought being a woman in a committed relationship with another cop wouldn't work.

He smiled. He would just have to show her how wrong she was.

He walked around the bottom floor of her brownstone trying to find out more about her. He toured the living room that was perfectly decorated with Victorian furniture and boasted a mid-eighteenth-century fireplace with a brass and iron fire grate.

He wandered into the formal dining room, the wall

painted a dusty blue. A huge dark walnut table with shaped feet made him stop and admire its highly polished surface. Someone had given it a great deal of loving attention. Six Victorian chairs sat around the oval table. He lightly ran his fingertips over the satin finish on his way to the kitchen.

The kitchen looked totally redone, with a lot of cabinets and updated stainless-steel appliances. A granite countertop ran the length of the cherry cabinets and a matching island with a double stainless-steel sink sat in the center of travertine-tiled floors. She had pots of herbs growing on the windowsill behind the sink. Trent imagined Linda leaning over and inhaling the scent of dill and sage. Not knowing exactly why, he pinched off a small piece of parsley and ate it and then laughed. It was a silly thing to do.

Beyond the kitchen was an office. Shelves lined one wall. The opposite was covered with pictures. One was obviously her father in his dress uniform. He was standing next to a woman he assumed was Linda's mother. The second picture was probably her brother and his wife. There was a similarity in his face; the same jaw, again the same eyes.

Trent went back to her father's picture. He was a handsome man and stood about six inches taller than her mother. From it, he could see that Linda had his eyes and the same smile he loved to see on her. There was a great deal of her mother in her too; the same soft curve of the jaw, the same nose. He thought the mix of inherited features was perfect on Linda.

The next photo was a picture of Linda in full dress. She looked a lot younger and Trent guessed that it must have been taken when she graduated from the Police Academy.

He slid back the pocket door on the far side and found himself in the study. He jerked to a stop when he saw Linda there still on the phone. He took a step back and started to close the door.

"It's okay," he heard Linda say, "I'm just finishing."

He stayed silent while she ended the conversation and hung up the phone.

"What do you think of the house?" she asked him.

"It's great. Whoever decorated it has impeccable taste."

"Mom did," Linda replied.

Trent nodded in admiration. He gestured over his shoulder. "I snuck a peak at your pictures." He took a step back as she walked by him into the office.

She ran her fingertips over her father's picture. "This one was taken at the firehouse just before they went to a dinner for the retiring chief."

"They look happy," Trent commented.

"They did their best," she replied.

"And this one," Trent said, pointing to her picture. "Graduation?"

Linda laughed and took it from the wall. "We all have one like that." She looked at it. "All spit and vinegar. Ready to go out there and get the bad guys." She shook her head. "Totally unprepared for the reality of the job."

Trent took it from her and hung it back in its place. "We should all hold on to that idealistic feeling we had at that time. It's something we need to get us over the tough spots."

Linda nodded and looked down at the floor. "In a perfect world."

"Is this you?" he asked.

She looked up to find his palms braced on the top of the desk, head cocked to one side as he studied a photo in an oval frame.

"Yes it is."

He looked back at her and gave her a disarming grin. "You look cute with pigtails and freckles."

"Luckily I outgrew both."

"Too bad," he joked, turning his attention back to the photo and a string of others in line next to it. "You played tennis in high school?"

"Varsity in my sophomore year."

"I tried a hand at basketball and ran some cross-country track."

She put her hands on her hips and looked him up and down. "You aren't quite tall enough for basketball."

"What I lacked in height, I made up in speed."

"I'll bet. She smirked and pointed to the last picture in the line. "Center, also sophomore year."

Trent straightened and walked to it. It was a team picture with a championship trophy. "You were tall and lanky at the time," he acknowledged, picking her out in the photo with no problem.

"And you were average but fast by your own words," she countered.

"Tall enough to take you on in a one-on-one now." A mischievous light seemed to come up in his eyes. "And I'm slow enough when it counts."

"We are talking basketball," she countered.

"Perhaps."

"Cutesy innuendo won't work on me," Linda cautioned.

Trent laughed. "Never thought it would." He motioned over his shoulder. "The taxi's waiting. I better go."

"It's going to be quite a bill," Linda acknowledged.

"You're worth it."

"Anther line?" she asked, walking with him to the front door.

"The truth." He saw the appreciation in her eyes. He gave her a slight smile and took her hand. "Come here," he whispered. His left arm circled her just beneath the ribs.

His eyes flickered across her face from the thick wave of dark hair that fell onto her forehead, past the dark eyebrows to the sparkling blue of her eyes. It lingered there for a moment before continuing down to the sweep of her mouth with its full lower lip, and he knew there was no turning back now.

With a tug he brought her closer to him. "I'm going to kiss you, Linda."

"Looks that way."

"If you don't want me to, I'll give you five seconds to stop me." He tensed and stopped the forward movement of his head until it seemed just a breath away from hers. "Five . . ." His whispered countdown began.

Her gaze moved across his face, studying him. When it moved to his mouth, his smile showed her he would neither demand nor force her to meet him halfway in a kiss.

"Four."

She lifted her gaze and found herself pulled into the smoky hue of his eyes. The gentle stroke of his fingers on her skin shut off her mind that screamed out a warning.

"Three."

Heaven help her, she knew she shouldn't be encouraging him, but his warm breath against her skin sent a shiver along her spine.

"Two."

Okay, she'd let him kiss her. A quick little peck that would mean nothing and make him realize that she could only offer him friendship. That there would be nothing more offered that could be construed as her wanting a relationship with him. Yes, she thought, a peck. That would do it.

"One."

Her lashes swept downward and her lips parted slightly, waiting for contact with his mouth. She took a quick intake of breath, preparing herself to kiss him quickly and move away. But the touch of his heated mouth on hers brought back a rush of memories and instead she surrendered to the promise she felt in his kiss, a promise that this time would be more than what they had shared before.

He did not disappoint. He was masterful in capturing her lips with his. There was nothing tentative or searching about his kiss this time. Precise and potent, it told her exactly what he wanted from her and she knew a quick peck wouldn't do.

Despite knowing better, she couldn't seem to get enough of him. She devoured his kisses. The roughness of his face with the beginning of a sandpapery shadow of a late-day growth on his cheeks only heightened her excitement. She met and matched his need, lost in a series of molten liquid explosions that blossomed inside her.

Through the excitement that tingled inside her, her voice of reason began to slowly overpower the contentment. *This can't happen. You know it can't.*

She broke the kiss and pulled back. Through the haze of her excitement, she saw Trent stare down at her as he smiled a slow, sensual smile.

Now she'd gone and done it, hadn't she?

But she didn't have time to answer her own

questions as a kaleidoscope of color exploded outside her front window. Blue, white, and red flash-
ing lights pulsating like a computer panel gone tilt.

A short siren blast preceded a booming but static-
sounding voice, "Move your vehicle, cabbie. It's
blocking traffic!"

Trent and Linda broke out of their embrace. "I forgot about the cab," Trent said, turning quickly on his
heel and tearing open the front door in time to see
the cab's red taillights stop at the corner. He took the
front steps of Linda's brownstone two at a time and
hit the sidewalk just as the cab turned the corner and
disappeared.

Linda was right behind him. "I am so sorry. It's
all my fault. Come back inside and I'll call you another."

About that time the police cruiser pulled up next to
them. The driver opened the window. "Hiya, Wolff.
Was that your cab?"

Linda leaned onto the car's door. "Sort of."

"We got a call that it was sitting here for a half hour
with the motor running. Apparently it spooked a couple of your neighbors."

She put her hand on the door frame. "Sorry, Mack.
Bad judgment on my part."

Trent stepped next to her. "Actually, it was my
fault, Officer."

The officer tossed his head toward Trent. "Friend
of yours?" he asked Linda.

"Yes. She was showing me her brownstone and I guess I lost track of time," Trent answered for her.

Linda angled her head to Trent. "He wasn't asking you."

The officer looked from Linda to Trent, a grin breaking on his face. "Don't start a lover's quarrel on my account."

Linda forced a smile. "It's not a lover's quarrel. It's not a lover's *anything*," she said with emphasis. Mr. Archer here is a visiting officer from New Jersey."

"And you were showing him around your place?" The officer laughed. "Nothing of interest in there."

The officer's partner broke out into a hearty chuckle at the comment.

Linda dipped her head and got eye level with him. "Knock it off, Grossman."

Just then a radio call came in and the officer's partner acknowledged. "Received."

"Gotta go, Wolff. Duty calls." The officer turned on the overheads, shifted the cruiser into drive, and sped away, sirens blaring.

"Great," Linda said, crossing her hands over her chest and staring down at the sidewalk. "Can't wait to see what version of this hits shift."

"Does it worry you that much?" Trent asked as they headed back to her brownstone.

Linda shook her head. "Not really. It's more annoying than anything else. I'm sure it's not different in Hillsborough."

Trent laughed. "It's probably worse. You have a lot more going on in the city than we do in the burbs. We live for something like this." At the top step he reached around her and opened the door.

She stepped inside. "Come in and I'll call you a cab." She shifted from foot to foot and looked up and down the block.

Trent caught the nervousness in her body language. "I think the inside of your brownstone is not the best place for me right now." He saw her blush. "I'll catch a cab at the corner."

"You sure?" she asked him.

Trent reached out and touched her cheek with the back of his hand before smiling slowly and stepping back. "I'm sure that if I go back into your brownstone, it's going to be a long while before I even think about getting into a cab and going home."

Linda spent most of the night wide-awake, tossing and turning. When she did manage to catch some sleep, it wasn't the deep, restful kind that would prepare her for another hectic day on the streets of New York. It was the half-asleep, half-awake kind that gave her mind an excuse to make weird dreams out of her confusion.

How dare Trent kiss her like that? How dare he make things more confused than ever for her.

Why couldn't he be more like the men she worked with at Manhattan South, men who treated her more like one of the guys rather than a woman with needs. The guys she worked with saw her as competition. That she could handle.

Why in the world had Trent felt the need to come all the way to New York to talk to her when she had purposely blown off the wedding brunch? She thought he'd realize he'd been dumped and forget all about her. Apparently, though, he had gotten some other message.

She tried her hardest to figure out what happened, but mostly all she could figure out was that Trent Archer was playing havoc with her senses. Her nighttime imagination kept replaying some interesting scenarios about what may have happened if he did come back inside her brownstone for a while.

By the time morning light began to play with the curtains she was completely angry with him. And darn him to heck for making that kiss one that actually could have curled her toes.

She threw the pillow at her alarm clock as it went off. It hit the floor with a dull thud but continued to beep. She got out of bed and silenced it. Then she looked at herself in the mirror. Dark circles had formed under her eyes.

It was going to be one of those days.

Chapter Ten

"Where have you been?" Ali Archer said as soon as her brother opened the door to his townhouse.

Trent yawned and looked at the watch he always wore. "Mooch, it's seven A.M. and it's my day off. Can't this wait?"

Ali handed him the newspaper she'd picked up from the driveway and pushed passed him. "No. The grass is six inches high in my yard and the lawnmower's broken. I need to borrow yours."

He pulled his front door shut and turned to face her. "I have a townhouse. I don't do lawns. That's why I pay exorbitant association fees. To let someone else mow the lawn."

"Oh, I forgot."

"No you didn't. Why don't you just tell me why you're here?'

Ali threw herself down in an armchair. "Where were you all day yesterday?"

Trent stood in front of her, arms crossed. "How do you know I was anywhere?"

"Because I tried to call you a dozen times and kept getting your voice mail here at the house. So where were you?"

"Why do you want to know?"

"Because I have a bad feeling about you and your wedding partner."

"What kind of bad feeling?"

"You were a little annoyed that she didn't come to the brunch on Sunday."

Trent walked into the kitchen to get a cup of day-old coffee with Ali close on his heels. He poured the dark liquid into a chipped mug, put it in the microwave, and set it to Auto Cook for a minute.

"How can you drink that?" she asked, making a face. "I know your coffee. It could rot your gut on the first try."

He turned to face her. "Which question do you want me to answer first? Brunch or coffee?" The microwave pinged, signaling the coffee was ready.

Ali tossed her hand in the air. "Your choice. I probably won't get a straight answer on either anyway."

Trent took a small sip of the coffee to test its temperature. Satisfied it wouldn't burn a path to his stomach, he took a much healthier sized gulp before answering her.

"You're right. I was a bit annoyed that Linda blew off the party."

Ali slapped her hands together. "I thought so. You two were pretty tight at the wedding."

"She's all right," Trent said before filling his mouth with more coffee to prevent him from saying more.

"If you like macho female cops," Ali added.

Trent nodded. "She's not that macho."

Ali eyed him warily. "What do you mean by that?"

"Why do you want to know?"

"Do you have to always answer my questions with a question?"

"Is that what I do?"

She pressed her lips together and nodded. "Every time you don't want me to know something." She walked to the table and slid herself onto it. "So what is it this time?" she asked, swinging her legs. "Why won't you tell me where you were all day? I called your cell about a hundred times too."

"I was out of town," Trent said, draining his cup and walking to the sink. "And I turned my cell off." He rinsed the cup under running water and then put it on the top rack of the dishwasher.

Ali was next to him in a second. "You never turn off your cell phone."

Trent patted her on top of her head. "Well I turned it off this time."

"Something's fishy here," Ali said, squinting.

"Why do you say that?" Trent shut the dishwasher door and walked back into the living room. Ali was so close behind him that if they were in the sun, they would have only made one shadow.

"Mom had the feeling you went to see Linda," Ali continued. "She's convinced that she started a chain of events when she gave us Grandma Vicky's rings that will lead to her having tons of grandchildren. Kinda like a fall into an abyss."

Trent sat down on his recliner and opened the paper. "Maybe she did."

The paper in Trent's hands crumbled as Ali slashed through it like a ninja breaking a board with his hand. "What did you say?"

"I said, maybe she did."

Ali looked positively petrified. "What exactly do you mean by that?" She circled his chair like a vulture stalking its prey, and smacked him on top of his head from behind the chair. "You *did* spend the day with Linda yesterday, didn't you?"

Trent swatted her hand away just before she would have connected with his head again. "Not exactly the day," Trent corrected.

Ali's eyes widened. "You spent the night with her?" She ran to the staircase. "Is she hiding upstairs or something? Linda! Linda Wolff. Come down here. I have to warn you about something."

Trent stood, shaking his head. "She's not here."

"Where is she, then?"

"Catching the bad guys in New York, I suppose."

Ali strode over to her brother and smacked him on the arm. "Don't get cute with me. What did you do yesterday?"

"You're just full of questions, aren't you?"

"There you go again. Answering a question with a question." She plopped herself down in his recliner. "I'm not moving until you tell me what's going on." She looked down at the armrests. "Yuck. Do you ever clean this thing?"

Trent brushed some crumbs from the right armrest. "I like it just fine the way it is."

"Okay, so we've established that you're a slob. Where were you?"

"I went to the city."

"To see Linda."

"You'd make a great detective, Mooch."

"I can do without any sarcastic comments from you, big brother. Why?"

Trent sat on the sofa opposite her. "Because she missed brunch."

"And you thought she might be hungry? What did you do? Bring her a cold plate of eggs?"

"No. I just wanted to know why she didn't come."

"You could have called her."

Trent leaned forward and rested his forearms on his thighs. "I needed to see her."

Ali bolted to standing and swatted at the air. "Oh

no, you didn't. Needed? Did you say needed? That's not good. I mean she's cute and everything, not as muscular as I thought she would be, being a city cop and everything. She's more curvy. But needed? You *needed* to see her?"

Trent had to concentrate his gaze on his sister to get his mind off the word *curvy*. Linda was that, all right. He remembered vividly how she felt when he held her. He blinked a few times to clear the thought and instead focused on something a bit less enjoyable. Like the police interruption of their evening.

"Yes," he told his sister. "I needed to see her and find out why she blew off the brunch."

"Was it that important?"

Trent stood and walked to the front window. Ali's eyes followed him there. "Yes it was."

She let out a long breath of air. "This is so not good."

Trent turned back to face her. "It was nothing, Mooch."

"Define nothing."

"I saw her, we talked, and I came home."

Ali shrugged. "Sounds harmless enough. Besides, I don't think it would work out between you two."

"Why not?"

"She'd cramp your style, Casanova. Most of the women in town are in love with you. You wouldn't want to break their collective hearts all at once, would you?"

Trent cocked a dark eyebrow at her and shrugged. "Not all of the women in town are in love with me."

Ali laughed. "Probably not. Probably they only pretend to be interested in you to get out of a ticket or something."

Trent laughed. "Some of them try that tact, but I don't fall for it much. Although I have to admit, I do like the attention."

Ali clapped her hands together. "There you go. You don't have to go all the way to New York to find a date. Just wait behind the sign at the high school until some cutie runs the light."

"Not my style, Mooch."

She waved away the comment. "Doesn't matter. You're not going to see Linda again, are you?"

Trent shrugged his answer.

Ali narrowed her gaze at her brother. "We pinky-promised. Those rings aren't going to get us, right?"

A slow smile worked its way across Trent's mouth as he escorted his sister to the door. "That was your plan, Mooch." He leaned over and kissed her on the cheek. "Your plan."

Linda checked her duty weapon before placing it back in the holster, buckling it around her waist and retrieving her hat from the top shelf of her locker. Muster for morning shift was in ten minutes. Then she shut her locker and spun the lock.

"When's Nick coming back?" Pat Vaughn, another

female cop just finishing getting ready on the other side of the bench asked her.

"I think he and his new wife went to Hawaii for their honeymoon," Linda told her. "He'll be back a week from Friday."

Pat's locker shut with a bang. "I always hate it when my partner goes on vacation. Teaming up with a sub isn't the same."

"I know the feeling," Linda agreed, checking the radio mike attached to her shoulder.

"Bet the six months Nick was out on medical leave seemed like six years."

Linda nodded. "More like sixty," she confirmed. "But I thought he'd be out a whole lot longer with what happened."

Pat swiped at the air. "Naw, he's a tough one that Daultry. You knew nothing would keep him down long." She laughed. "Who would have guessed that a stint in the Cop Swap would take him out though." She shook her head. "Darn shame someone that fine is married and off limits." She adjusted her belt. "I never got the chance to ask you. How was the wedding?" She laughed again. "I'd a paid anything to see you in a gown and high heels."

"Very funny, Vaughn. It was good," Linda returned. "Good to see Nick so happy."

"Yeah, it was a rough couple of months there. He deserves it."

As Linda walked to roll call with Pat, she could

not help but let her mind drift back to the day Nick got hurt. She could still not shake the feeling that it had been her fault.

She remembered it as though it had only been yesterday instead of almost a year ago. She and Nick were on the night shift patrolling the Theater District. It had been an uneventful night and the last show had let out almost two hours earlier. They turned the corner in the cruiser about three blocks north of Times Square when they saw someone who looked like he had been propped up against a subway entrance.

Nick shined the exterior light on the man, but he did not move. Next he clicked on the overheads and eased the cruiser to the curb. He told Linda to wait near the car until backup came, but she hadn't listened. She had only taken a few steps toward the sidewalk when the guy jumped up and attacked Nick. She ran to help him, but by that time a group of kids came pouring out of the steps of the subway entrance and joined the fray.

She had only a moment to react and pull out her nightstick before three of them came at her. Swinging it in a wide arc, she connected with a few arms and chests before Nick managed to break away from the punks on him and turned to help her. A few of the punks had what seemed to be some type of club. One or two of them landed some good blows to her arms, but the vest she wore under her uniform kept them from doing any damage to her chest.

She saw Nick land a few good shots of his own as one of the kids tried to get at his gun. He did a good job of angling his body so it stayed out of reach, as did she, but they were out numbered, and she thought they were going to go down.

The scuffle seemed to go on forever before an approaching siren could be heard in the distance. She had turned toward the sound when one of the punks landed a heavy hit to the side of her head. She stumbled backward and slumped against the building.

She remembered Nick calling her name and felt a pair of hands take her and toss her to the ground. She remembered feeling a heavy weight on her chest and looking up into a pair of dark, angry eyes right before the punk seemed to fly off her. Another pair of hands picked her up from the sidewalk and tossed her back into the police cruiser just as backup screeched to a halt in the street.

There was a glint of silver in the glow of the street-light and then the sound of retreating steps breaking into a run. As her head began to clear, she could hear shouts and cries for someone to radio for an ambulance.

She got out of the car to tell them she was all right when she saw Nick down in the street. A fellow officer was kneeling beside him, hand on Nick's chest and calling for assistance. Nick had been knifed.

It was the one time since she became a police officer that she had been truly scared. Not for herself, but for her partner. Nick was down and it was all her fault. If only she hadn't gotten out of that car.

Pat's voice slowly came into Linda's mind like someone had turned up the volume. "Hey, you okay?"

Linda gave her head a barely perceptible shake. "Sure. Why?"

"I asked if you knew anything about the girl who caught Nick and you had this weird look on your face."

"I'm fine, I'm fine," Linda replied, walking into the roll call area and taking a seat in the back.

Pat sat down next to her. "So do you?"

Still reeling a little from the memory, Linda did her best to concentrate on Pat's question. But the vision of Nick down in the street still remained. "Do I what?" she finally said

"Know anything about the girl who nabbed Nick?"

Linda nodded. "She's a nice girl. He really loves her. They'll be fine."

Pat pulled out her notepad. "Knowing what I know, seeing what I've seen, I don't think I'd want to be married to a cop," she said. "Especially not a city cop."

Linda could hear Pat rambling on about danger and punks and guns and laws, but her own mind was underscoring her decision. Trent Archer was a thing of the past. She made a mistake once, a mistake that almost cost her partner his life. Couple that with the loss of her father on 9/11 and she knew that she could not make another one by having a relationship with someone in an equally dangerous job as her own. She could ill afford the distraction. No matter how attractive that distraction might be.

The shift commander's voice snapped her out of her deliberation.

"Good morning, boys and girls," he said, shifting through the papers on the podium in front of him. "Let's see what the city has in store for you today."

Chapter Eleven

Ever since he had kissed her that night at her brownstone, Trent found himself spending a lot of the downtime on his shift thinking about Linda. He couldn't help it. Although he couldn't put his finger on exactly why, he knew he had moved beyond being curious about her. He was at the wanting-to-know stage, escalating quickly to the realm of needing-to-know.

Especially after all the fun he had kissing her the night before.

He needed to know what the slow looks he caught her giving him meant. He needed to know what she liked to do for fun. He needed to know why she seemed so dead-set against exploring having a relationship with him. Why couldn't he be this interested in someone less complicated?

Then he really needed to know what would happened if he made it a whole lot more complicated.

So he came up with a plan. In the last few hours of his shift, he had formulated a detailed plan to make Linda let down her guard and let him find out whatever it was that seemed to be creating a barrier between them.

Of course he needed to keep in mind that pressing her might just scare her off, but he could handle that. He had a plan.

Planning was something he was comfortable doing. It was a guy thing. Trent always started everything with a good, well-thought-out plan. It was part of his police training. On the job a guy knew how things worked, where everyone was supposed to be, and how it was all going to come out. If you stuck to a plan, you got results.

If all worked according to his plan, he would have a whole lot more one-on-one time with Linda. Once she got to know him better, he was positive she could not resist the old Archer charm.

"Linda Wolff," he whispered as he turned into the parking lot at Hillsborough PD. What was it about her that rooted her so deeply inside his head?

He was certainly attracted to her, that was for sure. He couldn't help it that her beautiful blue eyes filled him with a sense of contentment what he'd never know with another woman. Or that her dark hair reminded him of polished ebony. Or that her laughter made him want to listen to its rich tone longer than necessary.

He shook his head. He really liked her. She was a woman who knew herself, who used her spirit to accomplish anything she would set her mind to. There was so much going on in those eyes of hers that he knew it would take a lifetime for him to get to know it all.

If only he could find a big enough crack in the wall to wiggle through and get inside.

The plan, he reminded himself. Stick to the plan.

He signed out after his shift, changed in the locker room, and headed for the nearest florist. Ordering flowers for Linda was something he was not going to trust to a phone call.

Order flowers in person. Step one in the plan.

"Wolff, delivery!"

Augie's voice carried through the intercom in the locker room like he was screaming.

Linda went over and pressed the talk button. "What is it?"

"Come up and find out," came the crackled reply.

"Augie, come on. What is it?"

"Guess."

She could hear tinny laughter from those near the desk. Okay, she thought, she'd play along. "Give me a hint."

"I'll give you three. It's yellow, has thorns, and it's making me sneeze."

Linda's last thought before she let go of the button was *No he did not!*

But he had. Perched on the corner of the shift commander's desk were a dozen yellow roses. Augie saw Linda immediately. He pinched his nose. "Get these outta here before they kill me. Tell your boyfriend to send your flowers to your house."

Linda took the flowers from his outstretched hand and read the card. *Sorry about the cab thing. I'll make it up to you, Trent.* She shoved the card into her pants pocket.

"Sorry, Augie," she said walking away. "You'll be able to breath better in a minute."

"Take this other thing too," he called out to her.

She turned back. "What other thing?"

"You got two deliveries, Wolff."

He waited until she walked back to the desk before reaching down and pulling up a two-by-two-foot metal street sign. "They guys at the 7-1 thought you might need this." He held it up for everyone to see, and read: "No parking this side." Some wise guy had added in black marker: "unless you're visiting Wolff."

Linda shook her head and took it from him as the rumble of laughter rolled down the hall. She could feel the heat of embarrassment rise on her skin.

"Just great," she mumbled. "Didn't take them long."

"Why so upset?" Augie asked. "The guys just wanted to make sure your boyfriend didn't block the street next time he comes over."

"He's not my boyfriend," she countered.

Augie pointed to the roses in her hand. "Then maybe you ought to tell him that."

Linda looked from the flowers to the wide-grinned faces of everyone around her. "I intend to do just that."

Back at her house, Linda put the roses in a crystal vase. As she ran water into it, she had to admit, they were beautiful. It wasn't Trent's fault that she would be the object of some joking for the next few days. She had been the one to invite him inside.

The kiss that kept him there had been all his fault, though. Sure, she may have enjoyed the way he felt and tasted. She was, after all, only human. Girls like to kiss guys every now and again. It's part of what makes the world go around. But he knew the cab was outside and he knew that she had made it clear that she was not interested in a relationship with another cop.

Hadn't she?

Well, if she hadn't, then she sure would make sure the message was loud and clear when she called him to thank him for the flowers.

She put the flowers on the table in the kitchen, softening her stance as she looked at them. Not very many men sent her flowers lately, and they were beautiful.

Closing her eyes, she tried to strengthen her resolve. Don't fall for it, Linda, she warned herself. He may be charming, intelligent, funny, and a whole lot more rolled up in a mighty fine package, but that was no reason to deviate from the plan.

What plan? She put the heels of her hands over her eyes. She had no plan. She knew she had to call him and thank him for the flowers. It was the right thing to do. If she kept the conversation short and to the point, maybe she'd even come away from it with her wits still intact.

Why then were her hands already sweating?

Chapter Twelve

The phone only rang twice before Trent answered. "Hi, Trent, it's me, Linda."

She paused as he acknowledged her. Lordy, he had a great voice, she thought. Its rich baritone timbre wrapped around her like a blanket, making her feel all warm inside. *Stay on point,* she reminded herself. *Don't let those strong tones distract you.*

But as he continued talking, asking her how her day had been, she felt a resonance that seemed to make her heart jump. This was not going anything like the way she had planned it and all he said so far had basically been hello.

"I had a good day," she told him. "Ran down a purse snatcher on 44th near the Penn Club, caught up on some paperwork and, oh, I got some nice flowers."

She laughed in response to him asking her "From whom?" "From Brad Pitt. Who else would send me flowers?"

She listened to the deep character of his laughter in response to her playful question and tried to figure out a way to stop time so she could listen to it forever.

"Thanks," she told him. "But it wasn't necessary."

He told her that he felt responsible for the ribbing she probably had to endure from him showing up at the precinct and for his stunt with the cab. He knew how the guys at his job looked for every possible opportunity to poke jabs at anyone who gave them an opening, and he hoped it hadn't been too awful.

"Well, I did get another gift," she admitted. "No, Brad didn't actually send me anything. The guys from the 71st did."

She paused again while he rattled off a litany of apologies.

"Aren't you going to ask me what they sent me?" she asked him.

She smiled when she heard him say that he was a little afraid to.

"They got me a No Parking sign."

She heard him laugh with relief.

"I'm not done," she cautioned. "They added a little editorial comment with a black marker. It said, 'No parking this side unless you're seeing Linda Wolff.' "

Silence alternated with attempts at stifled laughter

on the other end of the phone until laughter finally won out.

"Unfortunately, I have to agree with you," she told him. "It was good, and I would have done the same thing given the chance."

They talked for a few minutes about mundane things like whether or not she had been able to audit the class he'd made her miss, whether either of them had heard from Nick and Somer, and what each other's plans were for the weekend.

"I supposed Nick and Somer have more important things to do than worry about us," she said. "Hawaiian sunsets are supposed to be beautiful, and I imagine that sharing them with the one you love makes them even more spectacular."

She actually felt herself blush when she heard Trent say that maybe they'd be able to experience the same thing someday. But feeling the warmth crowd into her cheeks also probably had something to do with the acceleration of her heartbeat in reaction to his words when, for a brief moment, she visualized them on a beach watching the sun set in a pastel sky.

"I want to thank you again for the flowers, Trent," she said, wrapping the phone cord around her forefinger as she tried to decide whether or not to invite him to New York for—

For what? she asked herself. To encourage something that she would ultimately have to end if it got too comfortable and he got too close? She inhaled deeply and set her resolve.

"Take care of yourself," she heard herself say right before she disconnected the call.

For a long moment she just stood there, receiver pressed to her ear as though she were still waiting to hear Trent's voice. Then slowly, she replaced the receiver in the cradle and walked away.

Though Trent Archer had come awfully close to getting her to let down her guard, she could not let him inside her head.

Doing so would be too dangerous for her heart.

"Linda I'd like to—"

Then there was dial tone.

Trent didn't have time to say anything before Linda hung up the phone. He had been planning to ask to see her again. She hadn't given him the chance, so she left him no choice.

He pulled open the drawer to the mahogany desk in his office and rummaged through a few papers before he found the train schedule. Then checking his watch he calculated he had about a half hour to get to New Bruswick in time for the next train. If he hurried, he just might make it.

It had taken longer to get to Brooklyn than Trent estimated. It was well past 7. The train to Penn Station had been held up and then there was the endless cab ride from there. He paid the cabbie and sent him on his way. There'd be no surprises from Brooklyn PD tonight.

As Trent stared up at Linda's brownstone wondering what he was going to say, a few kids he gauged were all around twelve or so came around the corner across the street. They passed a basketball around as they walked.

"Hey, guys," Trent called out, checking the street before jogging toward them. "Wait up."

They seemed to stop in unison. "What you want, dude?" one of them asked.

"Is there a park around here?" Trent replied.

The tallest one tucked the basketball under his arm and pointed down the street. "Three blocks that way."

Trent gestured to the basketball. "Does it have a court?"

"Why, you up for a game?" one of the kids asked. He looked around. "Where's your team?"

"Don't exactly have one," Trent replied.

"You thinking about a one-on-one?" the kid asked.

"Naw, he's too old, dude," another said.

Laughter erupted and Trent laughed along with them. "I agree."

"Then watcha want, dude?" the tall kid asked again.

Trent lifted his chin. "How much you want for the basketball?"

The tall kid looked at his friends before looking back at Trent. "Twenty bucks," he said.

"Thirty," one of the kids shouted.

"No forty," said another.

"Tell you what," Trent said, "I'll give you fifty."

The kid holding the ball looked skeptical. "What you want it for?"

Trent crooked his finger and beckoned the kids closer. "I want to impress a girl."

The kid made a face and held out the ball. "With this?"

Trent nodded.

"You'd be better off with flowers or something," the kid said.

Trent laughed. "I tried that. It didn't work."

The kid looked at his friends again before holding out the ball. "It's your money, dude. Fifty."

Transaction done, Trent watched the kids leave in the direction of the park. He bounced the ball a few times before tucking it under his arm and jogging back across the street.

When he got to Linda's townhouse he took the stairs two at a time. At the door, he took a deep breath.

"Here goes nothing," he said right before he pressed the doorbell.

The sound of her doorbell at this hour of the evening surprised Linda. She wasn't expecting anyone.

Frowning, she turned off the television and headed for the front door. Who could it possibly be?

Opening the door, her lips parted. "Trent." His name came out in a whisper. She looked from his eyes to his lips and back to his eyes. Her breath caught. His eyes seemed to hold her fast to the spot. Then suddenly the twinkle set in the corners of his eyes seemed to brighten and she became marginally aware of a rhythmic tapping sound.

She finally managed to tear her gaze from his incredible eyes and realized that he was bouncing a basketball on her stoop.

"Hi, Linda," she heard him say. "Feel like shooting some hoops?"

Chapter Thirteen

The park was just down the street from Linda's brownstone, one of the few in the area. As they walked toward it, Trent bounced the basketball in time to his steps. As she studied him, she noticed how intent he was on making sure he didn't miss the ball when it sprang back from the sidewalk to meet his hand. She almost laughed at the concentration on his face.

He turned his head and caught her looking at him. He smiled. She smiled back and pointed to the ball. When he went back to his focused dribbling, at that moment Linda realized something incredible. She could actually share silence comfortably with Trent.

Most men she knew would not be satisfied with just bouncing a basketball while they walked down to the court. They'd have to be talking about something—the last Knicks game, the time they'd made a three-pointer in a pickup game they played the weekend before, something competitive or assertive. Something that began to establish the male-female roles.

It was nice to be with someone who was content to just smile and be with her.

"I find it hard to believe that you came all the way to Brooklyn to play basketball," she said when they got to the court.

"You did say you were a champion in high school," he said with a slanting grin. He opened the chain-link gate and let her go inside first. As she turned to face him he threw her the ball. "Prove it."

She caught it easily, surprised her reaction time was still good. She bounced the ball a few times. "I haven't done this for a few years," she admitted.

"Want to warm up first?" he asked her.

"Yes," she replied, turning and heading for the far basket.

He watched her glide easily down the court, eyes on the net, bouncing the ball in front of her, before taking two steps and easily completing a layup.

"You don't seem too rusty," he noted.

She tossed him the ball. "Let's see if you are."

Trent snatched the ball from the air and headed in the opposite direction, mirroring her move. When he leaped and shot the ball, he intended to bank it off the backboard, but instead it caromed off the rim and to the right.

"Maybe I'm the one who needs the practice," he said, retrieving the ball as it rolled to the fence.

Linda stood center court and waited for him to join her. "Shall we shoot layups for a while? Until we warm up?" she asked.

He nodded and tossed her the ball. They took their positions opposite each other.

"Ready?" she asked.

"Whenever you are?" he returned.

She made a run at the net and easily made the shot with Trent right there to catch the basketball as it cleared the net. Between then they made about twelve runs each before Linda finally missed.

"You're pretty good," Trent said, dribbling as he came back to center court.

"Guess I'm not as rusty as I thought," Linda replied honestly. "But then again, I haven't played against many guys either. Not too many want to go one-on-one with me."

Trent's smiled widened as he took off toward the net. "I do."

This time he made a move on the net that would be more difficult for her to rebound, angling his body so it crossed in front of the net so she would have to grab the ball from the other side. He barely had time to watch her form before she was sailing past him on her way to the basket.

They concentrated on an exchange of shots, each one scoring in an exchange of offense that lasted longer than the first series. This time, he was the one who missed the layup.

She bounced the ball a few times after she retrieved it. "Shall we begin?" she asked, standing on the center court line.

"Think you've warmed up enough?" he returned.

"I have."

"Then so have I." He stood in front of her, stance wide, bent slightly at the waist, hands out in a defensive posture.

She bounced the basketball a few times more, never taking her eyes from his. "Ready?"

He shifted his weight from foot to foot, getting ready to react to her move. "And I have to warn you, the fact the you're a girl doesn't mean anything. I intend to beat you."

Her smile came with a snicker. "Just the way I like it," she said right before faking a move to his right and then quickly moving to the left. She was past him before he could even react. He reached her side as the unmistakable sound of a basketball hitting the net sounded. "That's one," she said, catching the ball as it cleared the net and tossing it to him.

"You need twenty more," he reminded.

She was now on the defense. "I guess I need to get the ball back quickly." She glanced up at the sky. "It's getting dark."

He wore jeans and a T-shirt but Linda could see his muscles harden and square with each step he took. He pivoted and so did she, making sure she kept her body between him and the net. He planted his feet and weighed his next move and she was nearly undone by the way she saw the muscles in his forearms contract when he pulled the ball away from her.

Taking a step back, he jumped and arced the basketball over her head and easily into the net. He put out his hands and took a small bow. "Nothing but net."

"Okay, you got me on that one. But it won't happen again," she assured.

She took the next three points before he faked a move and made a perfect left-hand shot over her shoulder.

She raised an eyebrow and nodded appreciatively. "The man gets serious. But it's still four to two."

"Not for long." He walked to center court and began dribbling the ball.

She stood in front of him, knees slightly bent, hands resting on her thighs. "Face it, Archer. You got nothing."

Trent stopped dribbling, caught the ball, and stood straight up. "Not yet I don't," he said right before he took off toward the net.

She stood right where she was and let him score. Partly because he had been looking into her eyes when he made the comment and partly because his crinkle-eyed smile seemed to brighten up the fading light. But mostly because his intended double meaning hit her right in her heart.

After that they threw their total effort into the rest of the game. The score tied and then the lead changed hands three times over the next few minutes. They ran and reached and jostled each other in a rivalry that was more fun than competitive.

They were well matched. Physically Trent had the edge, but Linda was quicker. When he gained the lead by charging and muscling her out of the way, she responded by moving by him so fast that he did not have the chance to react. He had a more accurate long-range shot, but she was deadly right under the net.

They both seemed to revel in the exhilaration of pushing their bodies to physical limits. The air at the park was filled with the sound of rubber slapping on the court surface, the bounce of the basketball, the sound of the ball hitting the rim and the rattle of the backboard.

They darted and drove and sometimes watched the ball roll off the rim so slowly that they didn't know who would recover the rebound until the last second. Their shirts became moist and their arms glossy with moisture. His hair curled a bit near his hairline and hers got stringier. They smiled and laughed and teased. They shouted "Take that" and "Are you tired yet?"

And he took the game 21–20.

Trent walked to the bench near the chain-link fence and sat down. He rested his head against the fence and stuck his legs straight out. He closed his eyes. This victory was not as satisfying as most, but he knew Linda wouldn't respect him unless he gave 100 percent to the effort.

He lolled his head to the side and opened his eyes. Linda stood about six feet away from him using another bench for balance and stretching out the muscles of her right calf. She looked sensational.

She'd worn a pair of navy sweatpants with a white stripe down the sides. That little stripe now curved down her hip in a way that accented the toned and tapered muscles, drawing his eyes to the sensual curve of her legs. Her white NYPD T-shirt, now damp with moisture, clung to her, almost teasing him with the way it accented her form.

Strands of hair escaped the ponytail she wore. As he studied her, a breeze caught some of her loose hair and blew it across her lips. Without breaking her stretch, she hooked it with her little finger and pulled it back. Almost immediately another breeze came and sent it back across her face. This time she spit it out and then tucked it behind her ear.

Other women he knew wouldn't be caught dead doing something like that. At least not when they were out with him. He smiled. But Linda wasn't other women. She was real. Confident. Interesting as all get out.

"Hey, Wolff," he called out. "You're not bad."

She switched feet and angled her head to him.

"Neither are you. But next time I'm going to beat you." She walked to the bench and sat down next to him. "Thanks for not going easy on me."

"Would you have wanted me to?"

She shook her head. "No."

He leaned his head back against the fence and closed his eyes, his breathing become less labored as he rested. He felt the fence move and guessed she had rested her head on it too. He opened his eyes and found he had been right.

For a while he just admired her profile. Her up-turned, cute little nose. Eyelashes, the type women say were normally reserved for a man, shadowed her cheek from closed eyes. A tiny rivulet of moisture ran down her forehead, across her cheek, and down her neck. It took all the willpower he possessed not to trace its path with his forefinger.

"Quit staring at me," she said, eyes still closed.

"How do you know that I'm staring?" he asked.

"Because I'm a good cop."

She turned toward him. When her gaze locked with his, Trent felt himself nearly drown in their sky-blue depths. He saw so many emotions swirling there that he almost found it hard to speak.

"Tell me what you're thinking, Wolff."

She closed her eyes momentarily. "How do you know I'm thinking?"

He traced her brow with his forefinger. "I can feel it."

"I don't think you'd want to hear it."

"I think I should."

She started to say something but then retreated. "Never mind."

With a sigh, Trent sat up. "How am I supposed to 'never mind' when I care about you? I care about your thoughts, how you feel. I can't 'never mind.' "

Linda straightened so she could hold his gaze. "We're alike and we're opposites. Does that make sense?"

"Not too much about us makes sense."

She angled her body on the bench to face him, tucking one leg behind the other. "We're both cops, so we're both focused, confident, and capable."

"And that's a bad thing?"

"But we're not the same."

"Oh?"

"You take a more relaxed look at life. All I see is responsibility."

"So we'll counterbalance each other. That's a good thing."

She stood and began to pace. "When I'm with you I feel so—" She stopped, obviously looking for the right words. "So free to be myself. It's something I haven't felt for a long time. But we've only known each other for such a short time that it's also unnerving." She stopped walking and stood right in front of him. "Does that make any sense to you?"

He stood and put his hands on her shoulders,

partly to reassure her, partly so she wouldn't walk away from him. "Sure does. I think we're good together."

She didn't say anything, just looked in his eyes.

"I can feel you thinking again. Want to let me in on it?"

"I don't know what to do about it."

"For starters, we can meet in the middle. I can teach you not to take things so seriously and you can teach me how to act more responsibly." He felt her stiffen and shake her shoulders slightly before running his hands down her arms to take her hands in his.

"I didn't want to like you, Trent," she said, sounding as though she was forcing out the words. "But somehow you're getting to me. I don't know how or why, but you are."

"I'm flattered."

She shook her hands free. "No, you're not. You planned this. I know it. You came to my job, you sent me flowers, and you showed up on my doorstep in the middle of the week with a basketball."

He raised his hand, his thumb and forefinger about an inch apart. "Maybe a little planning went into tonight."

"I can't do this, Trent." She walked away from him.

He caught up with her in two strides. "I'm not asking for all that much, Linda." She turned and he saw doubt in her eyes. "Look, we all have the same fears. Police officers maybe even more than average people. There has to be a way for us to at least be friends. Can we start with that?"

Linda crossed her arms over her chest and looked down at the ground. Painful seconds went by without a word from her. He couldn't lose her now. Not when he was so close to convincing her that he was right for her.

Looking back at him, he saw the intensity in her eyes. "I think," she said softly, "that maybe we should take this one day at a time. If I look at who I am, I get uneasy about straying from the plans I made for myself, the solitary plans. And when I look at the future, my imagination runs wild and I think if I let someone in and then something goes wrong, I may not be able to cope."

"I know it won't be easy," Trent agreed, "but if we keep talking about things then we can dispel any fear you might have." He took her hands again. "What do you think?"

The beginning of a smile fled across her lips. "I think you could probably sell the proverbial ice to Eskimos."

He felt his own smile widen. "The only thing I want to sell right now is you on us. When I saw you that day at the church at the rehearsal for Nick and Somer's wedding, something happened to me. You stood out from the crowd. You were so confident, so independent, so beautiful. From that day on you kept coming into my mind. Then I couldn't get you out of my dreams. Now I don't want to."

Linda dipped her head. "I'm in your dreams, huh?"

He took her chin with the tips of his fingers and lifted it so he could meet her gaze. "Sure are."

"Want to tell me about them?"

"Not yet. We're still only at the talking stage, re-member?"

Linda nodded. "Trent, I can tell you where this may be going. I can't make any promises."

"And I won't ask for any. Just yet." She started to say something, but he silenced her with a finger to her lips. "I'm hungry. Are you?" He could almost see Linda relax with the change of subject.

"I am."

He angled his watch to his eyes. "It's too late for a big dinner." He looked up at her. "Do you have bread, cheese, a toaster, and a microwave back at your place?"

"I think so."

"Then you have everything I need to make it until breakfast."

Chapter Fourteen

The instant Trent stepped into Linda's townhouse kitchen whatever angst she had about him coming over instantly disappeared. He reached out to grab one of the knobs then stopped and wrinkled his nose. "I think I need to wash up a little."

"I was wondering when you were going to notice," Linda replied. She pointed to the hallway. "Two doors down on the right. I'll get you a clean towel and a clean shirt."

He nodded and she followed him into the hallway. He went right. She turned left.

From the closet in a utility room, she grabbed a sunny yellow bath towel, hand towel, and washcloth. Not knowing what he preferred she thought she'd take him all three. Then, opening a bottom storage drawer,

149

she rummaged through the T-shirts she kept stored there and brought out the only one marked XL. It was red, emblazoned with a PBA-sponsored ballgame ad but it would have to do.

She selected a light blue T-shirt in a smaller size for herself. Using the small sink in the utility room, she quickly washed up as best she could. She didn't want to waste time going up all the flights of steps to her room and doing a more complete job. It would take too long and she wanted to spend as much time as she could with Trent.

Satisfied that she looked more presentable, she draped the red T-shirt across the towels, scooped them up, and walked down the hall to the guest bathroom Trent was using. There she nearly dropped them when she saw him.

He was facing the window. The faucet was on full force, the sound masking her approach. She stood in the hallway, watching, careful not to let her reflection show in the mirror above the sink.

Trent stripped off his T-shirt and slung it across an empty towel bar. He picked up a bar of soap, bent over the sink and began scrubbing his hands and arms. He filled his cupped hands with water and splashed it across his face before he started cleaning the places he missed—his neck, stomach, under his arms.

When he leaned over the sink, she got a glimpse of the way the chiseled muscles of his back tapered to a slim waist. Her imagination sparked with a flash of what he might look like on the beach in a bathing suit, fueling a second vision of her being there with him.

She watched in fascination as he continued with his cleaning ritual. As he moved, the muscles of his back contracted and released, drawing her attention to his upper body. He wet his hand and ran it across the back of his neck, the hair curling there now wet and darker in color. Then he cupped his hands under the water again and slapped them onto his face, blowing out his nose to keep the water from going up us nostrils.

Linda clasped her hand across her mouth to keep from laughing. It was like watching a dog getting out of some water and trying to shake himself dry. Water was everywhere, on the floor, on the countertop, on the mirror, even on the window.

Trent straightened, eyes closed, and groped the air next to his right hip, searching for a towel that was hanging from a second towel bar. Linda stepped forward and quietly thrust one she had been holding into his hand. He squared his shoulders and began drying his face.

When he turned, the towel was till covering his chin. He stopped moving when he saw her and stared at her from behind the towel. The pause that followed was something like a slow-motion stop of time in an old movie. Two water drops rolled off his left elbow and slid down his stomach. For Linda they seemed to take a delicious long minute to get where they were going.

Then Trent moved the towel and dried them from his skin. "I didn't know you were standing there." His gaze followed hers. Her eyes were following his hands.

"I brought you clean towels," she said, her gaze moving up his forearms to the hard muscles at his shoulders. "I wasn't sure if there were any in the bathroom." She took in the light silky hair that drew her gaze to his chest, not covering it totally, just spread out enough to be interesting.

"There was one here," he said, nodding toward it. "You didn't have to bother. You could have waited for me in the kitchen."

"No bother," Linda replied. Why on earth would any woman want to wait in the kitchen when she could see a man like Trent wash up in her bathroom? She handed him the T-shirt. "Hope it fits."

He slipped it over his head, adjusting it as it flowed over his upper body. He carefully draped the towel he'd used to dry himself over the top of the shower rod. "Is that okay?" he asked, pointing to it.

Linda nodded. "It's fine. I'll get it when I do some laundry later."

Trent retrieved his T-shirt from the other towel bar and slung it over his shoulder. "Okay," he said, slapping his hands together, "I believe I owe you a dinner. Where's the toaster and the microwave?"

She pointed down the hall. "Kitchen, of course."

Trent walked through the bathroom doorway and swept his hand through the air with a flourish. "After you. I'm all yours."

As she lead him back to the kitchen she had the giddy feeling that he was. Or rather that he could be whenever she said the word.

In the kitchen she watched Trent pull open the door to her professional-size refrigerator and rummage through the drawers. "How can you find anything in here?" he asked, his words a bit muffled from his head being inside the huge top section. He leaned back. "Where's the cheese?"

"Center drawer," Linda replied, opening the bin in the drawer to the cabinet next to the stove and grabbing the white bread. She handed it to him as he passed her on his way to the center island.

He looked at it. "White. Supposedly not very healthy."

"But the best kind for grilled cheese."

Trent grinned at her from the opposite side of the island. "Especially for grilled cheese à la Trent. Toaster?"

She pointed to the cabinet behind him. "Middle shelf. Where did you get the idea for this?"

Trent pulled the toaster in and turned back, feigning shock. "Idea? Why, I'll have you know that this is a secret family recipe, passed down over the last"—he rolled his wrist and looked at his watch—"couple of days or so." He laughed. She laughed with him. "Actually, I kind of got lazy one day and didn't feel like pulling out the frying pan to actually do the grill part of grilled cheese." He took two slices of bread from the sleeve. "You may want to write this down," he said as he popped them in the toaster.

"Of course," Linda said, pulling open a drawer and after retrieving a notepad and pencil began to write. "Step one. Put bread in toaster." She looked up. "I think I got that. What's next?"

He crooked his finger and beckoned to her. "Come over here."

"Why?"

"Step two is very important."

Linda put the pad on the countertop and began to walk around the island.

"No," Trent said. "Bring a notepad."

She gave him a slanting grin and picked it up. She'd play along.

"Very important," he said when she joined him near the toaster. "The bread can only get to a certain shade of brown or else the whole gourmet dish is ruined."

"And just how do you know when the bread is toasted to perfection?"

Trent stuck his finger in the air. "You watch." He bent over the toaster. After a few seconds he tilted his head toward Linda. "*We* watch. Get closer."

Still willing to play, Linda leaned over the toaster with him.

"See?" he said pointing to the bread. "It's staring to turn tan."

Linda pulled her brows together. "Wouldn't it be easier to set the dial on the side to the color you wanted?" she asked, pointing to the control underneath the lever.

Trent chuckled. "But it wouldn't be as much fun, now would it?"

She punched him on the arm and straightened about the same time the toast popped up. Trent took the slices with two fingers and set them on a plate.

"Now we put a little butter on the bread." Which he did with a grand gesture. He set the knife on the edge of the plate and picked up a few slices of cheese. "What do you think? Three or four slices?"

"Four, I think," Linda replied. "I still have an artery that may not be clogged."

"Four it is, then."

Trent topped the slices with the other slice of bread and then set it in the microwave. "I'll let you do the rest," he said after staring at the front controls for a while. "There are too many do-dads and dials on this one."

Linda reached around him and pressed a few buttons. "How much time does your creation need?"

"Thirty seconds ought to do it," he replied.

Linda stood next to him. "Do we have to watch this too?"

"Only with safety glasses."

"Fresh out."

"Then I suggest we get two glasses of milk and wait."

She filled his request and slid the glasses onto the granite top of the island. Then she eased herself onto one of the stools and waited.

Thirty seconds later Trent took some mighty fine-looking grilled cheese out from the microwave. He cut it so it produced two perfect triangles and took one before sliding the plate across the island to Linda.

He waited until she took a bite. "So?" he asked. What do you think?

She chewed thoughtfully and nodded. "Not bad. Not bad at all."

"So now you know I can cook. Does that get me a few extra points?"

"Maybe" was all that she would admit to at the moment.

They finished their sandwiches in silence, the only sound in the kitchen that of Trent almost bouncing the glass back onto the granite when he finished his milk.

He could tell she had something she wanted to say to him. It was something in the way she breathed, as if she were rehearsing something in her head and breathing at the times she was thinking.

Sure enough when she finished her own milk, she bit her lip and looked intently at him. "Trent?"

"Yes?"

He kept his tone casual. He didn't want to sound prying or testing. He was afraid if he did, he'd put her off and she would revert back to silence. Then he'd never know what she was going to say and it would drive him nuts for days.

"I think we have to talk some more."

"About what?" he raised his eyebrows. He really wanted to hear this, but wanted to take it very slow.

"About all this."

"What about all this?" *Slow and steady*, he said to himself. *Let her talk.*

She sighed. "Give me a minute, will you?"

"Take all the time you need, honey," he said. He gestured to the refrigerator. "Want another grilled cheese?"

She shook her head. "This friendship thing. Do you think it will work?"

Trent gathered the dirty dishes and set them in the sink. "Why wouldn't it?"

Linda joined him at the sink and rinsed the dishes before putting them in the dishwasher. "For starters, it never did for me before."

Trent rested his hip against the line of cabinets. "But you, me, we can be pretty good together."

Linda faced him, mimicking his pose. "I suppose."

"Are you telling me that all my hard work, my

cooking, was for nothing?" She really knew how to make a guy feel confident in his plan.

"It's not that I'm saying no, Trent. It's just that us being together tonight hasn't really proven anything. Oh sure, we had a great time playing basketball, at least I did."

Trent took her hand. "I did too. When we were playing there, joking around, I watched the love of life come into your eyes. There's a woman there under that police presence. I know there is."

Linda stood very quiet, looking at her hand in his and digesting his words. She felt Trent's fingers move over her skin on the back of her hand in a caressing motion.

"That may be true, but I'm a police officer first." She looked up into his eyes. "I'm afraid that it's always going to be that way."

"Why can't you be both, a police officer and a woman?"

"If you have to ask that question, then you'd never understand the answer." She looked down and tried to pull her hand free but he would not allow it.

The urge to take Linda in his arms and tell her just what a desirable woman she was raced through him. He saw her lower lip tremble and watched as she bit down on it to hide the reaction.

"I'm sorry," he said. "Maybe I want too much too soon. Ali always accused me of plowing straight ahead after something I want and not looking around for the roadblocks. I guess she was right."

With a small, one-cornered smile Linda looked back up into his eyes. What she saw in his eyes was something she hadn't seen in a very long time. There was so much caring and warmth there that it seemed to break the very last chain she had around her heart.

"When I told you at the wedding that there weren't many second dates, I led you to believe that it was because of the competition at work."

"I remember," Trent said.

"That wasn't entirely true."

"Okay."

"I mean it is true, but the reason isn't."

"Go on. But only if you want to."

She nodded. "I do. I'm the one who usually cut it off. When dad died at the Towers, it tore Mom up inside really bad. She never recovered from it. She couldn't stay here in New York. That's why she moved to Virginia to be closer to my brother. For me it had the opposite effect. I threw myself into my work, afraid to slow down and take it easy. Afraid that if I did, I'd be somewhere else again when I was needed. I never totally understood why I did that," she admitted in a soft voice.

"I think you're trying to prove to everyone else and yourself that you're worthy of still being here even though you were thousands of miles away when it happened." Lifting his other hand, he moved several strands of dark hair behind her ear. "Trust me when I tell you, we all feel like that at one time or another."

"I never realized that." Tears glistened in her eyes.

"It doesn't matter. What matters is that you know that now. What matters is you."

"So you think there's hope?"

He moved his hands to her shoulders and gave them a gentle shake. "I know there is."

Linda smiled as though Trent were the sun and she was basking in the rays of his love. Her eyes widened. Love? Couldn't be. She quickly filed the word away for a time when she could think about it more closely.

"Maybe," she said. She turned and rested her backside against the cabinets.

"I'll just have to prove it to you then," Trent said, adjusting his position to face her with his hands on either side of her hips on the countertop.

Linda put her hands on his shoulders and looked deep into his eyes. His words were a powerful awakening to her senses and she was walking out onto terribly dangerous ground. She had meant to gently push him away but felt herself opening and closing her hands on his shoulders instead.

Slowly Trent's mouth began to descend toward hers. Linda kept her gaze on his, watching the emotions in his eyes closely. She saw hope there and genuine caring coupled with sparks of desire.

This time as he molded his mouth to hers, claiming her with fire, she felt his heated response build in response to hers. Her hands slid down to the front of his chest. A groan started deep inside him as kisses, one after another, mingled. Her world ground to a halt, the past fears forgotten, the future only a dream as she focused on the present and anchored there more firmly with each kiss.

She focused on his texture, the feel of his muscles beneath her fingertips and her blatantly female response to him. Each kiss was a step forward with trust.

Then slowly he broke his contact with her and opened his eyes. There was awe and desire in them. He managed a shaky smile. "Every time I kiss you, it feels so right," he said, his voice low and husky.

Linda felt breathless. She needed Trent's hands on either side of her hips to keep her from swaying. Never before had she been kissed with such tenderness but also with such a need that it made her feel like she was the only woman in the world.

"I—"

Trent put a fingertip over her lips. "Shh. Don't talk. Just feel." And then he kissed her again.

This time when they broke contact, they stood just looking at each other, inches apart, as the evening flowed around them. For her it felt so right. And if she cared to be honest with herself, she'd have to admit that almost from the first time she met him, it had felt that way.

The deep brown of his eyes spoke of his need for her

in such a way that it sent warmth spiraling down to her heart. If only he wasn't a—the thought began, but Linda banished it from her mind, at least for now. Tonight she wanted to enjoy him just as a man.

She studied Trent for a minute, not wanting to discuss the moment or what he might possibly mean to her. Maybe it was all a dream, a dream that would be gone in the morning.

"You're thinking again," she heard Trent say.

She put her hands on either side of his face and kissed him chastely. "How do you know so much?"

He saw the emotions in her eyes shift and figured it was the wall coming up again. He'd give her time to adjust to the way she reacted to him as a woman, but before he left her tonight, he'd make sure that she didn't forget it.

"Having two sisters, I've gotten a pretty good education on women's feelings," he replied.

"Thank them for me," she said. When she shifted her weight away from Trent, he let her go.

"What does your schedule look like for the next few weeks?"

"Why?" she asked.

"Because I want to see you again. "I'd like you to come back to Hillsborough. Maybe take you to dinner and show you life in a small town. I mean, tonight wasn't really planned. I'd like to take you on a real date."

Linda felt herself cringe with the word. *Date?*

Though she wanted to tell him yes, for some reason, she still hedged. "It's going to be a tight few weeks. I still want to take that class." She whirled around and started to move away from him.

He reached out and took her arm. "Are you running from me?"

Her eyes widened. The question struck home. "Running? No. I just have a busy next few days."

Trent shook his head. "I don't buy it. What we have is good. Solid." He pointed to his chest. I can feel it here. My heart doesn't lie to me and I don't think yours does either."

"You have no right to stand there and try to tell me what my heart does and does not say."

"Oh yes I do," he countered. "I happen to like you a heck of a lot. I like you bordering on a heck of a lot more and that gives me the right."

With that Trent pulled her into his arms. A sigh escaped her as she accepted his warm, hungry kiss. The contact with his body was electrifying. She felt his warm breath against her ear when he moved his kisses across her cheek and then returned to her mouth. They moved and kissed in perfect unison that it was almost as though they had galvanized into one.

Gradually Trent broke contact with her, their breaths mingling in a symphony of sighs as they stood, foreheads pressed against each other. His arms tightened against her and he nuzzled her hair before stepping back and smiling.

"Good night, Linda. I can see myself out."

"Good night," she said as he stepped back. Any other words lodged in her throat, blocked there by all the rich emotions Trent's kisses had made her feel. She wanted him to stay longer, but knew she was incapable of making a coherent decision.

So she merely watched Trent leave quietly without a backward glance. How long she stood there in her kitchen thinking of his kisses, she did not know. But when the clock struck midnight, she knew that she had to get some sleep. She had to get to work early the next morning and had to be ready and sharp for her shift.

First, though, she wanted to take care of the water splashes in the bathroom. She grabbed a few kitchen towels and headed there. A minute, that's all the time it would take, she decided.

But as soon as she entered, a mixture of lingering aromas assailed her and she stopped dead in the doorway. The soap he had used, an undertone of the scent of intense physical activity, the last remnents of damp towels, all brought back vivid memories of Trent and his kiss. Why she honed in on the traces of these scents, she didn't know. Logically, they should have been long gone, but there was nothing logical anymore about her building attraction to Trent.

She wiped the sink, inhaling the fragrance of the soap he had used and the memory of him shirtless flooded her mind. She gathered the towel he had used and lifted it to her nose. The scent of man and musk filling her head.

Lowering the towel she looked at the reflection in the mirror. "No sense fighting it any longer. You're falling in love with him."

Chapter Fifteen

The next morning, as Trent prepared for another workday, he felt really good about what he and Linda accomplished the previous evening. A huge barrier had been torn down, he thought. He'd taken it from her by simply loving her and not pushing too much.

Loving her. He rolled the words around in his mind. Yes, he did love her. And she loved him back. She just didn't want to admit it yet. He sensed her vulnerable state and wisely had not asked anything until she wanted to talk about her feelings.

Frowning, he hoped she didn't wait too long to realize what they could have. She needed time to assimilate and absorb it all and he knew it.

"There you are," one of the other detectives said. He tossed Trent the key to one of the unmarked cars. "Someone broke into the school last night."

Trent caught it with his right hand. "How bad is it, Sam?"

"Some vandalism in the school store, a couple of fire extinguishers tossed through some trophy cases, graffiti across some lockers. All more annoying than serious. The chief wants us to go over and talk to the principal."

Trent grabbed a new pocket-size notebook and stuffed it into his back pants pocket. "While we're there, let's check in with Kirby."

"The Enforcer?"

Trent laughed. "Yeah, he enforced the heck out of me when I was in high school, and with good reason. He's tough, but he's a good guy and the kids respect him. A lot of them come in just to BS with him, and he listens to every one of them. Sometimes on his own time. I bet you anything he already has a beat on who did this."

"That would be nice. I'm working the fund-raiser at the ball park tonight."

"Me too," Trent returned. "So let's get to the school and wrap this one up in record time."

"Hey," Sam said as they both walked out to the parking lot. "I hear you have a new squeeze."

"Working on it," Trent acknowledged, hitting the

button on the key tag and listening to the beep of the car door unlocking.

"When are we going to meet her?"

Trent opened the door to the driver's side and got in. "Working on that too."

"What's her name?"

"Linda. Linda Wolff."

Sam shook his head. "Nope. Not familiar with that one."

"She's from the city and she's blue."

"A cop?"

Trent nodded.

"Well, well, well, my man, that's interesting. How did you meet her?"

"She was in my sister's wedding."

Sam waved his hands in front of his face. "I hate weddings. You can always count on someone trying to hook you up if they find out you're single. The bridesmaids are all starry-eyed, the unmarried female relatives all want to be in the bride's place, and the mothers are always looking for men who could be husband material for their unmarried daughters." He slapped Trent on the shoulder. "Which one got you?"

Trent eased the car out of the parking space and onto the road. "It wasn't like that. Linda is my sister's new husband's partner at Manhattan South. We got paired up in the wedding party and hit it off."

"Are you sure she isn't looking for a husband?"

Trent thought back to his conversation with Linda.

"I'm sure of it," he said in reply. "But it would be a lot easier if she was."

A quizzical look rolled over Sam's face. "Huh?"

"Never mind," Trent said. "It would take too long to explain." He gestured to the sheet they'd been handed on the way out of the station. "We're almost at the school. Fill me in."

Trent's surprise at seeing Linda just inside the glass doors to the police station turned to pure pleasure. As he and his partner walked through the outer doors, he absorbed the way she looked. She wore a light blue boatneck top that deepened the color of her eyes enough for him to see her even from a distance. The urge to run his hand through her dark hair and take her in his arms was almost physical.

He waved to her and saw her waggle her fingers back. He could feel the smile break out on his face.

"Is that her?" Sam asked.

"Sure is."

Sam stopped. "From the look on your face, I'd say you were pretty serious about her."

"She's special," Trent admitted, a sudden catch in his voice. The depth of his feelings for her surprised even him. He kept walking straight for her.

His partner caught up. "She's pretty."

"I know."

"But then standing next to you, anyone would look good."

"Knock it off, Sam," Trent said right before he pushed open the double doors.

Sam stepped in front of Trent, standing right between Trent and Linda. "Hi, Sam Morgan." He stuck out his hand.

Linda took it tentatively. "Linda Wolff," she returned, looking over his shoulder at Trent. Trent just shrugged an "I don't know what's going on" at her.

Putting his hand on Linda's shoulder, Sam eased her across the room. "Can I speak to you for a minute, Linda?"

She furrowed her brows. "Sure," she replied as Trent still gave her no hint as to what may be happening. "What can I do for you?" She looked again at Trent just as she settled near the far wall of the reception area.

Sam turned and looked at Trent, who gave Sam an unmistakable warning look. "I just wanted to see for myself." He looked over his shoulder at Trent. "For purely investigative purposes, I assure you."

When he turned back to face her, the grin on Sam's face told Linda more than Trent ever could. This had something to do with her and Trent. She decided to play along. After all, hadn't she been the subject of some good-natured ribbing when Trent had come to Manhattan South and waited for her to get off shift?

"And what do you see, detective?" Linda asked him.

"I see that Trent was right."

She looked over Sam's shoulder and saw Trent striding quickly toward them.

"That's enough," Trent said, taking Linda's hand as soon as he got close enough to reach it and pulling her around Sam and away from him. "Linda didn't come here to be the subject of one of your idiotic investigations."

"I don't mind, Trent," Linda said, stopping and walking back to Sam. She held out her hands and turned in a small, tight circle. "So? Do I pass muster?" She saw Trent's shoulders sag.

"Ten-four on that," Sam replied.

"Glad you approve." She walked over to Trent and took his hand.

"She's a keeper."

Trent squeezed Linda's hand. "Working on it."

"Try not to screw it up," Sam advised. "But if you do, get me her phone number."

As Sam walked away laughing, Trent took Linda into a small room where all the reports were written. He wanted to kiss her, but not in front of everyone. Maybe he'd get the chance in there.

"Sorry about that," he said, looking through the window back out into the hallway to make sure Sam wasn't lurking somewhere outside the door.

Linda chuckled and put her purse down on the table that was set in the center of the room. "He's harmless."

"I don't want you to think everyone on the Hillsborough force is like Sam."

She waved away his concern. "Boys will be boys, Trent. They are no different at NYPD. I don't mind. It releases the tension of the job." She took a step closer to him. "I gathered that you told him about me." She tilted her head and gave him a analytical stare. "What did you tell him?"

He stepped closer to her, pleased she didn't step back. "I told him that you were pretty."

She looped her arms around his neck, amazed at how comfortable she felt doing it. "Just pretty? Not amazingly beautiful?" She felt Trent's hands settled onto her hips.

"If I told him that, I'd never get him to leave." His gaze ambled over her face before settling on her eyes. "But you are amazingly beautiful."

She had only meant to tease him, but the serious tone of his voice and the intent look in his eyes told her that he meant every word. Without thinking about whether there would be consequences, she leaned into the hard male lines of his body and let his mouth capture hers in a welcomed kiss.

She inhaled his masculine scent, a faint whiff of perspiration mixed with a stringer aroma of citrus aftershave. When he moved his head she felt the faint sandpapery scratch of stubble against her skin. As she surrendered to this exquisite assault on her senses, the words *I love you* were almost torn from her. She swallowed them. It was too soon for her to say something as important as that. She wasn't totally sure she could give him everything that came with those important words. Not yet. When she said them to him, if she said them to him, she would have to be 100 percent sure she was ready to accept the responsibility that came along with those words. Reluctantly she broke contact with him.

"Well that was a nice surprise," he said planting small kisses on her brow, cheek, and nose. "Not that I'm complaining, but what brings you here?"

Linda rested her head against his cheek, content to listen to his slow, even breathing. "You asked me to come to Hillsborough." She stepped back away enough to look into his eyes. "I thought I'd take you up on it." When Trent took his hands from her hips, she moved her arms from around his shoulders.

"I didn't mean for you to hop on a train the next day." He took her hands in his and gently ran his thumbs across the back of her hands.

"You're busy today." She looked down at his hands holding hers and then back up. "I feel so stupid. I'll call a cab and get on the next train home."

Trent kissed her fingers. "No, I want you here. It's just that I would have come to New York to get you."

Linda felt herself relax. "So it's okay?"

Trent squeezed her hands. "It's more than okay. I just hope you're flexible."

"I am so flexible," she assured. "Did I tell you that

I was also the gymnastic champion of the fifth grade?"

"That's not what I meant. I have to work a fund-raiser at the ballpark tonight. It's too late to find someone to fill in and it won't be over until about ten."

"What kind of fund-raiser?"

"Every month the PBA takes over the concession stands at the ballpark for one of the games. Ten percent of everything sold that night goes to an organization called Operation Shoebox to help the troops serving overseas. It's a partnership with the baseball team, the concession contractor, and the PBA."

"Nick's cousin is in Iraq."

Trent nodded. "I heard that. Nick told me that his cousin would have been in the wedding party, but he deployed the week before."

"How long is his tour?"

"He's on his second, actually."

"Impressive."

"And courageous," Trent added.

Linda didn't hesitate. "So can I help?"

"You wouldn't mind? We could do something later, if there's time before the last train back to New York."

"Or we could so something another day," Linda suggested. "This fund-raiser is important, and I really would like to help out."

Delighted, Trent looped an arm around her shoulders. "You are amazing. I'll make it up to you, I promise."

Linda picked up her bag from the tabletop. "Nothing to make up. Just sell a lot of hot dogs tonight, Archer, because I plan on making this the best night ever."

As they walked out of the room and into the hall, in that instant, Trent thought that maybe by the way Linda smiled at him, maybe she didn't mean it would be the best night for the fund-raiser.

Chapter Sixteen

"**H**ey guys, this is Linda," Trent said, walking around the counter to the serving area, holding Linda's handing.

A chorus of "Hi, Linda" greeted her.

"Hi, guys," she acknowledged. "Hope you don't mind another pair of hands."

A sandy-haired man looked up from filling a cooler with ice. "That would mean Archer will have to let go of one of yours."

Laughter filled the space. "Very funny, Nolan. Just keep your hands off hers."

"What do you want me to do?" Linda asked.

"Besides stand there and look gorgeous?"

Linda turned to the familiar voice. "Hi, Sam. We meet again."

"Did you have to bring him?" Sam asked, gesturing toward Trent.

"I think so," Linda replied, tying on the apron Trent handed her.

"And she cooks!" Sam exclaimed. "If I knew that, I would have arm-wrestled Archer for the honor of bringing you here."

Linda laughed.

"Ignore him," Trent said with a smile. "He doesn't get out much, so he doesn't know how to talk to a lady."

"Why don't you and your girlfriend man the french-fry station?" an older, white-haired man asked. "One of you fries, the other serves, okay?"

Linda turned to Trent. "Okay by me. Which do you want?"

Trent was already pouring oil into the fryer. "I'll cook, you charm the customers into buying extra."

Over the next few minutes Linda organized the paper containers for the fries, while Trent turned up the heat and began frying his first batch of potatoes. After a few minutes he dumped a pile of golden brown fries into a metal warming tray.

After generously salting them, he took one between his thumb and forefinger and blew across it. "Here, try one," he said, holding it out to Linda.

"Grilled cheese and fries," she noted, taking a small bite from the fry he offered her. "We'll die young from clogged arteries and cholesterol, but at least we'll eat."

"Gather round everyone," the white-haired man said. "Instruction time."

Linda and Trent joined a group of six men. As they listened to the instructions, Trent put his arm around Linda and pulled her against his hip. She turned her head to him and smiled. He winked back at her. The simple exchange of gestures sent a warmth through her. It felt so right, so comfortable to be with him. She'd known him for a just a few weeks, but it felt more as though she had known him for a lifetime already.

As Trent listened intently, she watched him. Warmth flowed through her just seeing him smile. Trent's confidence, his poise, and the way he let his emotions show awed her. With him she could be a cop and a woman and it didn't matter.

She wondered briefly if all the stories she'd heard about knowing when you found the person who was right could be true. Because she felt as if she probably just had.

They worked nonstop it seemed from the time the gates opened. The only break they got was when the national anthem played and when the home team paid tribute to the service men and women in attendance. Even when the mascots played games to engage the fans and keep them interested between innings, it seemed the food lines stretched five-deep.

"Two large," Linda called out, taking the money handed to her.

"Copy that," Trent said, scooping fries into the paper carriers.

Linda took the two orders from the warming trays and turned back to the counter. Her customer had taken a step to the left and she now stood face-to-face with Trent's sister Ali.

"What are you doing here?" Ali asked, absolute horror on her face.

"Trent, look who's here," Linda called back to him, handing the fries to her customer.

"Hey, Mooch," Trent called out when he saw his sister. "How many do you want?"

"Never mind that," Ali said. "Why are you here, Linda?"

"I came to see Trent and he talked me into helping out with this fund-raiser."

"I can see that," Ali countered. "But shouldn't you be in New York catching some bad guys or something?"

"It's my day off."

"What are you doing with my brother?"

Linda almost laughed out loud at the look on Ali's face. "Selling fries," she replied instead.

Ali sighed. "I mean, are you *with* my brother?"

"Hey, you gonna order something or not?" a guy behind Ali said.

"Diet Coke and some fries," Ali said before spinning around and giving him an annoyed look. "Happy?"

"I can help you here," one of the other officers behind the counter said. The man moved over and placed his order.

"What was the question again?" Linda asked, pressing a lid onto the top of the soda.

"You know very well what the question was. You just don't want to answer it," Ali whispered.

"Here you go, Mooch," Trent said, sliding an extremely large plate of fries onto the counter. "Personal delivery for my little sister."

Ali reached over the counter and grabbed his shirt. "What are you doing? Why is Linda here?"

Trent pried his sister's fingers from his shirt. "She came to visit."

"Why?"

"Because she likes me."

"How much?" Ali asked, looking from her brother to Linda.

"Enough to come to Hillsborough from New York on her day off."

"Does Mom know about this? She's here, you know."

"Where?" Trent asked.

"Upstairs in one of the suites."

"Tell her to come down."

"No!" Ali cried, her eyes widening. "She can never see you and Linda together."

"Why not?"

"Because of the ring," Ali said, her voice a whisper. She looked around, scanning the area like a spy. "If she sees you and Linda together, she'll think she did it. Then the pressure is on me."

Trent laughed. Linda snickered. "You know I don't believe in that," he assured.

"Doesn't matter. She does. Is that ring still in your sock drawer?" she asked.

Trent nodded.

"Make sure it stays there," Ali warned. "Don't look at it. Don't touch it. Don't even think about it." She turned her attention to Linda. "No offense intended, of course."

"Of course," Linda acknowledged.

"I'm sure you're a very nice person, but you can't have a thing with my brother. You understand, don't you, Linda?"

"I'm not sure I do," Linda said with a grimace.

Ali picked up the fries from the counter and looked from Linda to Trent. They were looking at each other with something other than amusement on their faces.

"Oh, this is not good," Ali could be heard mumbling as she walked away.

In the seventh inning, she and Trent were able to rotate out of working for the evening. A few people from the local firehouse came in to take over.

"Let's watch the game for a few minutes," Trent

suggested. "Unless you want to go somewhere else?"

Linda looked at her watch. It was nearly 9:30 P.M. "I have to catch the eleven P.M. train back to New York. It's probably better if we stay here. There's a station right behind the stadium. I can pick it up there."

"I'm going with you," Trent said without hesitation.

They sat in two empty seats in the last row of the lower-tier seating. "It's not necessary," she said. "I just have to catch the connection at Newark and get a cab from Penn Station."

"It may not be necessary, but it's the right thing to do. I'm coming with you until I put you in a cab. Then I'll catch the next train back."

"I am capable of doing it alone. I am a police officer, you know."

"Being capable has nothing to do with it and I am well aware of the fact that you're a police officer. I just don't feel right letting you go home alone."

"How can I be sure that you won't follow me home in the next cab?"

Trent shrugged. "You can't."

Just the sound of the bat connecting with a fastball made Trent jump to his feet and cheer. Home run. The home team went ahead by two. Linda watched him high-five a few of the fans around him before settling back down in his seat.

"I didn't know you were such big a fan," she said.

"I am," he said, putting his arm wound her shoulder and pulling her to him. "Of the team too."

Linda smirked at the obvious double meaning, but settled comfortably into his side. The next two batters struck out and the seventh inning ended. As the home team took the field, changing from offense to defense, she never noticed the cameraman who had settled right in front of them.

She did, however, take notice of the hooting and hollering around her. She looked around and saw that some fans were pointing at her and Trent while others were pointing at the scoreboard. They all had one thing in common, however. They were shouting, "Kiss her!"

Linda looked up and found that she and Trent were on the Kiss-cam. The cameraman was shooting a live shot of them and it showed up on the scoreboard inside a big red heart.

Trent looked at it and laughed. "The only way we're going to get off that scoreboard is for me to kiss you, you know."

The chant got louder. "Kiss her, kiss her." And the cameraman zoomed in closer.

"Your mother's going to notice this," Linda warned.

"She was going to find out sooner or later," Trent said just before he did what the crowd was instructing.

Hours later, Trent's cell phone rang. "You're home. Good," he said after answering it and hearing Linda's voice. He paused. "I think I have about three stops left before Bridgewater. It's a short drive home from there."

He smiled as he listened to her. "I had a great time too. Can I call you tomorrow? Great. Linda, I—" He stopped and edited his words. "I'm glad you came."

Linda pressed her head against the tiled wall of the shower stall listening to the spray echo through the glass enclosure. Her eyes were closed as she let the warm water flow over her shoulders.

How could she possibly have fallen this fast and this hard for a man she had only met such a short time ago? The questions had no real answers, yet she distinctly recognized the powerful attraction between them. It had been such a short time, yet with each day that passed, it left her more and more certain that they were destined to be together.

She lifted her head and took a step back, letting the warm water hit her hair. The shampoo she used smelled of lavender as she worked it through her long dark hair, wickedly imagining it was Trent's fingers massaging her scalp. What had he done to set himself so firmly inside her mind?

Nothing, she decided. Nothing but simply being himself and allowing her to do the same.

She got out of the shower, dried and wrapped a towel, turban-style, around her head, securing it at the nape of her neck. After she dressed in a simple cotton nightgown, she sat at her dressing table and brushed the tangles from her wet hair.

Thoughts of Trent flooded her mind.

Fixed inside her head now were daydreams of his soft brown eyes with thick lashes that made his eyes more striking than a man's should be. Just thinking of the way his bottom lip pushed forward when he was deep in thought made her break into a wide grin. There was no good reason to deny it any longer. She wanted him all for herself.

Trent Archer was an incredible combination of strength and gentleness, caring and grit. That unique blend made her heart beat faster at the mere thought of him.

She dried her hair quickly and got into bed. She pulled the thick green blanket up and tried to think of something other than him. But it was useless. Every time she attempted to block out his image, it came swimming back in front of her eyes.

She sighed heavily and decided not to fight it. She closed her eyes and waited for the dreams of him she knew would come.

Chapter Seventeen

"What would you like to do today?" Trent asked, talking to Linda on his cell phone as the train rumbled to a stop at Metro Park in Edison. "I should be at Penn in about twenty minutes." He watched a few passengers settle on their seats as Linda talked. "Let's be tourists today," he suggested. "In the three months we've been sharing time between New York and New Jersey, we've never done something like that." When she agreed, he looked at his watch before continuing. "Why don't we meet at Sarabeth's at Central Park South for brunch at eleven. Great. See you there."

Trent ended the call and tucked the phone into his inside jacket pocket. It had been an amazing few months. Using some creativity and some compromises, he and Linda had managed to pack a whole lot into juggling their days off, work schedules, and being a bi-state couple. Occasionally he stayed at her brownstone in her brother's room and less often, she stayed in his townhouse in the guest room. He didn't ask her to stay over much, but instead, planned a lot of their time together making sure they ended up at or near her place at the end of the evening.

But this date was going to be different. He was ready for a deeper commitment, and sensed she might be leaning in that direction also. It was time to let Linda know just how serious he was about her.

He reached into his pants pocket and pulled out the ring. Holding it up between his thumb and forefinger, he let the morning light shining through the train window catch the sapphire facets, producing tiny stars among the deep blue color of the stone. Stars like those he could see more often in Linda's eyes the more time they spent together.

His mom told him that the sapphires promote harmony and loyalty. That would help him with consistency and reliability to the woman he ultimately chose to share his life. He'd brushed off his mother's pronouncement as girly voodoo, but since meeting Linda, everything the sapphire in his grandmother's ring was supposed to do actually happened.

Could have been coincidence, could have been karma. He didn't know which and didn't really care.

He planned on giving the ring to Linda, telling her that he loved her, and letting her decide.

Linda waited outside Sarabeth's for Trent, eagerly scanning up and down the street for any sign of him. Right across the street a line of hansom cabs took on and discharged passengers. All the time she'd been in New York, she'd never ridden in one. Maybe after brunch she could talk Trent into really being a tourist.

She leaned against the building and watched diners go in and out of the restaurant. She'd taken the day off to spend it with Trent. Normally they managed to fit seeing each other into their crazy schedules, but this week, she wanted one normal weekend day with the man she loved.

The man she loved?

Wow, it was the first time she'd thought that without first justifying the words. They came so easily too. She didn't feel scared or jumpy or ready to run away from then.

The man she loved.

Trent Archer was the man she loved.

She closed her eyes and inhaled deeply. And today she'd find the perfect time to tell him just that.

He saw her standing outside the restaurant. "Linda!" he shouted, waving his hand high so she would be able to see him among all the people walking on the sidewalk. She waved back and he cut across the street, carefully dodging cars and horses.

When he got to her side, he put his arms around her and kissed her. "You look great." He hugged her tightly. "Feel great too. Been working out?"

She laughed and punched his shoulder. "The only workout I get lately is a mental one trying to figure out my schedule, your schedule, and the train schedule."

"My algebra teacher said I'd thank her for making me pay attention." He raised his chin. "Thank you, Mrs. Anderson."

Linda joined his chorus. "And Mr. Whitestone."

They laughed and walked arm in arm to the restaurant. Despite being crowded, they managed to get seated within fifteen minutes at a cozy table in the back but by a window so they could still see the street. They ordered off the menu instead of opting for the brunch buffet and, after ordering and getting their coffee, they settled in to enjoy a leisurely breakfast.

Trent reached across the table and took her hand after she replaced her coffee cup in the saucer. "It's been an amazing few months, Linda."

She watched his thumb circle her knuckles and wondered how she ever got through a week without feeling his hand holding hers. "It's been more than amazing," she admitted.

Brows dragging downward, Trent said quietly, "At first I was always afraid that when you came out to see me that you were going to tell me it's over and it wasn't ever going to work out between us. I know how hard it was for you to put your fears aside and just try this."

Reaching out with her other hand, Linda took his between both of hers. "If it makes you feel any better, I almost did a few times." She saw Trent's eyes widen and felt is hand flex. "There were so many times that I stood there teetering between the joy of seeing you and the fear that one wrong move could take you away from me forever. But every minute we spent together only made be realize how happy I am when I'm with you."

Trent took her hand and kissed her knuckles. "That's only one of the many things I like about you. You're logical and can recognize a good thing when you see it." He smiled. He could not imagine himself with any other women. "And as far as something happening, it won't."

"It could, Trent."

He nodded. "But, honey, we can't live our lives on possibilities. I could slip in the shower. You could fall down the stairs. Anything, anytime could happen to anyone. We're not ostriches and we can't live our lives with our heads in the sand."

His sensitivity was one of the things she loved about him almost from the beginning. "Funny how we all have our fears, isn't it?"

He squeezed her hand. "Yes, but it's how we handle them that counts." He let go of her hand and dropped his chin. Now was the time. He reached into his pants pocket and curled his hand around the ring. "Linda, I can't imagine myself without you anymore."

"It's starting to be like that for me also," she admitted.

He began to pull out the ring when suddenly the sound of silverware tapping on a glass filled the room. They turned to the sound.

Two tables over, a young man of about twenty-five or so was getting down on one knee. His girlfriend looked like she was going to faint. "Rosie," he said, taking her hand. "I love you and I want to spend the rest of my life with you." He reached into his jacket pocket and pulled out a black velvet box, which he held out to her. "Marry me," he said, pulling open the lid.

His girlfriend squealed with delight and grabbed the box from his hand. "Yes!" she cried, jumping to her feet. "Yes, yes, yes!"

The room seemed to explode with shouts and applause as the young man put the ring on the finger of his fiancée. Trent looked at Linda who was beaming and clapping along.

Trent shoved his grandmother's ring deep down in his pocket. He could never top that in a million years.

As soon as they walked out of the restaurant, the idea hit Trent. He'd give Linda the ring during a ride through Central Park. He'd told her he wanted to be touristy today. What was more touristy than a ride in a hansom cab?

He gestured to them. "How about it?"

Linda nodded her agreement. "Why not?" They crossed the street and walked to the first one in line. "If you can believe it, I've never been in one of these."

Trent paid the fee for the "Lovers Loop" tour that would take about forty minutes and take them in a large ring in the park. He figured that somewhere around Bethesda Terrace, he'd asked her to take the ring. But if the moment wasn't right, he'd wait for Cherry Hill with its beautiful storybook-like vista. He waited until the driver settled Linda in the seat before he sat next to her.

"The horse is beautiful," Linda said as the driver eased the horse to a slow trot.

"Someday when we have time, we can go to Lancaster County in Pennsylvania. You can see tons of horse-drawn carriages there because there is such a high concentration of Amish in the area."

"Never been there, either," Linda replied.

"We'll have to remedy that."

They entered the park and began the steady ride along the pathway. Trent slid as close to her as he could and arched an arm around her shoulders. Linda took his other hand in hers.

For a while they rode like that in silence, holding hands in the sunshine. Children ran around the open areas, throwing balls and playing tag while parents or babysitters watched carefully from benches. A few couples had spread blankets on the grass and were either talking, reading, or snuggling.

The carriage came alongside a white-haired couple walking and holding hands. The man tugged on his partner's hand and pointed to the carriage. The woman looked at it, pressed her free hand to her chest in a loving gesture before waving to Trent and Linda. The man whispered something in her ear and she turned and kissed him on his cheek.

Linda waved back at them. "Isn't that adorable?" she asked. "They look so happy."

Now, Trent's mind screamed. *Lay the groundwork for the big event.* "Imagine what we'll be like when we're their age. Do you think we'll be walking in Central Park holding hands?"

"Are we going to be walking in Central Park holding hands, Trent?" she asked him.

"I said *imagine*," he countered.

"Okay, let's see. You'll be bald and I'll have short, white hair." She grinned. "I'll be wearing a hat all the time too."

"A hat with a big rose on the side."

"Maybe. We'll wear sensible shoes and matching warm-up suits because of the elastic waists."

Trent looked over at a woman pushing a baby carriage. "We'll just have come back from visiting our grandchildren."

"So we're married, then?"

"Have been for forty years."

Cherry Hill was long behind them as was Strawberry Fields and the lake. In fact, they were fast approaching Tavern on the Green so the ride was nearly over. It was way past time.

Linda furrowed her brow. "We couldn't possibly be married for forty years. There's not enough time for that. Thirty maybe. Thirty-five if we hurry."

"So I guess we better hurry," he said, reaching into his pants pocket.

About the same time, screams cut the air, getting closer and louder with each stride the horse took.

"Stop him! He has my purse!"

A man carrying a large black handbag ran right toward them. He crossed directly in front of the path of the horse as he headed for the edge of the park. The driver barely missed him as he brought the carriage to a stop. Behind him a women tried to keep up, frantically screaming and waving her arms.

Linda bolted to her feet and was out of the carriage in an instant with Trent right behind her. "Call 9-1-1," she called back as she took off running, following the path the purse snatcher had taken. "Tell the operator the suspect is headed down 65th West toward Trump Tower."

Trent pulled the phone from his pocket and caught up with the frantic victim. He settled her onto a bench to let her catch her breath and made the call just as Linda instructed.

"Stay with her," Trent told an officer who had been running about fifty feet behind the woman. The officer nodded and Trent took off running after Linda.

He found her four blocks down with the suspect on the ground. She'd pinned him there against the sidewalk with a knee to his chest, gun drawn. The siren in the distance became louder and more distinct, telling him that backup was close.

He ran to her. "Linda, are you all right?"

"Stay down. Put your hands on your head and don't move," she instructed the suspect as she rose. She tossed her chin toward a trash can. "He threw the purse in there," she told Trent.

Trent retrieved the purse and handed it to the patrolman who just got out of the cruiser that had arrived.

Linda took a step back and watched another officer handcuff the suspect and pull him to his feet. She lowered her weapon and put the safety back on as she holstered it behind her back.

"Where'd you come from?" the suspect asked as he passed her on the way to the patrol car.

"We'll take it from here," one of the officers said. "But you'll need to come down to the station and file a report."

Linda nodded.

Trent took her by the shoulders and urged her away from the gathering crowd. "What were you thinking?"

"I was thinking that I had to stop him."

"You could have been hurt."

"I'm fine."

"But he could have had a gun."

"But he didn't."

"That's not the point," Trent said, anger in his voice. "There was an officer right behind the victim and—" He stopped. What on earth was he saying? He would have done the exact same thing under similar circumstances. In this case, however, Linda had beat him to it. He pressed his lips together and just looked at her.

"I guess our date is over," she said to Trent.

Trent stuffed his hand into his pants pocket and cupped the ring. "I guess it is."

Trent sat on a bench in Central Park watching the sun set. He'd been there for hours although it seemed more like minutes. He didn't go with Linda to the station when she left to fill out the report. She didn't want him to. After his outburst, he couldn't blame her one bit.

She was a police officer, just like him. He would have expected nothing less of himself than the same reaction that she had if he'd seen a crime in progress. Why was it then that he thought for a fleeting moment that she should have left the chase for someone else?

For maybe the first time since he met her, he understood what she meant when she told him that she was afraid of a relationship with him. It wasn't that she was afraid of commitment; she was afraid of loss.

Today he felt it too. When she jumped out of the hansom cab and took off after the suspect, it was as though she had taken his heart with him. He had been afraid. Afraid of something happening to her. Afraid of losing her forever.

And now that he understood that, it was up to him to prove to her that the only way they could be safe was with each other.

Linda sat in the kitchen of her brownstone at a table drinking coffee and crying. She looked up and could almost see Trent leaning against the sink getting ready to kiss her. She dabbed at her eyes with a paper towel. Bet she'd never have to worry about whether or not she'd let him kiss her ever again. Surely not after today.

She had run down a purse snatcher and made a great bust. But in the process, she also snatched her future right out from her own hands. She was a cop; she couldn't be anything else. She proved that to him today.

Somewhere outside in the street, a car horn blared. Then another and another until the horns became so consistent that she had to get up and find out what was going on. As she got closer to the front door, she heard voices too.

"Linda! Linda Wolff! Are you in there? Linda Wolff, if you're in there, I love you! Come to think of it, even if you're not in there, I love you!"

It was Trent.

She ripped open the front door. Trent stood in the middle of the street, hands out to the side, blocking traffic, screaming at the top of his voice. On either side of him, cars were backing up until the line nearly reached the corner. Horns were blaring and drivers were shouting at him. But he refused to move.

He saw her a second later. "Linda! I love you," he shouted, but he still did not move from the center of the street.

She ran down the steps and stopped at the curb. "You're blocking traffic."

"I know. I thought that if I simply knocked on your door, you'd ignore me and wouldn't let me in."

"Trent, you know it's not a good idea."

"I'm not moving until you let me in and we talk."

Horns began again. "Let him in," one angry driver shouted. "My take-out is getting cold."

Trent raised his hands. "Your neighbors are going to call the police again. Wonder what they'll bring you this time?"

Linda strode into the street and pulled him to the sidewalk by his arm. "For the love of Pete, okay." She yanked him up the stairs. "Two minutes. That's all you have."

"I only need one," he assured her. He stopped at the entry foyer. "What are we going to do?" he asked her.

She opened her mouth to say something, but instead only a sob came out right before the tears. "I don't know." She turned and walked into the sitting room with Trent right on her heels.

When he caught up to her, he took her shoulders and turned her to face him. "When you took off after that suspect, I thought I was going to lose you."

"See," she said through her tears. "Now you understand."

He took her in his arms. "I do. Maybe for the first time."

She closed her eyes and her lids trembled. When she opened them, he saw the turmoil she faced. A terrible hurt grabbed his heart like a giant fist.

"But do you really think I could ever let you go now that I've found you?" he asked her.

She leaned her head on his shoulder and cried. He held her, allowing her the time she needed to calm before he urged her to look at him.

"I want to say marry me, Linda. I think that's what I want. But it happened so fast with you and I think that's the problem for both of us. We need some more time together, more time than we've had. Time for us both to understand that we need to be together. Time for us to explore that possibility. I'm thirty years old. I've waited a long time to find the right woman and I don't intend to let her go now just because she's afraid of loving someone."

"I don't want to lose you either, Trent."

He had been stroking her cheek with his thumb, but with her words he stopped. The seriousness of their gazes became so powerful that she had to close her eyes against the intensity.

"Look at me, Linda," Trent said, shaking her gently for emphasis. She opened her eyes. "I love you. I want to spend forever with you." She started to speak but he stopped her with a light kiss. "I know you think I take things lightly at times, but I take those words very seriously. I've been in some serious relationships, and I've come close, but I vowed never to say that to someone until I meant it." He looked straight into the blue eyes he loved so much. "And I haven't said it to any other woman before today."

Her lips opened and a hint of more tears sparkled in the corner of her eyes. "And I love you, Trent."

He rested his forehead on hers. "Finally," he whispered. His thumb caressed her lip before he slowly eradicated the space between their mouths, kissing her gently.

He pulled back. "I can't promise to give you the next minute, or hour, or day, or year. I don't know what's in store for us. I can only promise that I will give you my heart every moment of every day we have."

She closed her eyes and took a deep breath before opening them again. "I'll take it," she said.

"There is one more thing I can give you," he said, reaching into his pocket. "This." His fingers uncurled from around the sapphire ring.

A smile spread across Linda's lips right before it turned into a deep chuckle. "Who's going to tell Ali?"